TALES TOLD IN GASCONY

TALES TOLD IN GASCONY

Le Campagnol

Illustrations by Karen Pain Kort

MERLIN BOOKS

First published in Great Britain 1995

Published by Merlin Books Ltd.
Braunton, Devon, England

British Library Cataloguing in Publication Data.
A catalogue record for this book is available from the British Library.

ISBN 9 86303 720–8

Printed in England by Orchard & Ind Ltd., Gloucester

Contents

Introduction
Gascony and the Gascons

Gascony, that ancient region of France bordered by the Pyrenees, the Garonne and the Atlantic, was a sixth-century Basque creation. In 1036 it was united with the kingdom of Aquitaine, so one might wonder how it still manages to claim an existence at all. But these are not people to be forgotten so easily.

As part of Aquitaine, Gascony enjoyed the era of friendly warring with the English. The wine trade, it is interesting to note, continued throughout the period. Perhaps this has something to do with the fact that it is said today that it would be perfectly normal for the English to come back to this, their former home. However, grandmothers still tell naughty children that the Black Prince will come for them in the night if they do not mend their ways.

The French have their own opinions of Gascony. On the one hand, everyone knows that d'Artagnan was a Gascon, on the other, north of the Loire few can tell you where the region is located.

The native French dictionary defines a Gascon not only as a person from that region, but also as a 'trumpeting braggart', a 'speaker of vainglorious exaggerations'. The character of Cyrano de Bergerac sweeps to mind. A '*promess de Gascon*' is defined as a fantastic promise which is impossible to keep, and a '*gasconade*' is a witty pleasantry at best, a conceited boast at worst.

Gascons, needless to say then, were always ready to throw themselves into battle. Thus Gascony became a main source of French soldiers in its time. Sadly, the Franco-Prussian and First World Wars probably buried the best of Gascon manhood. The region was never to recover from this depopulation.

During the Second World War, one branch of the Resistance hoped to create an independent state of Occitana after the war. At that point Gascony was still bilingual, clinging to a regional dialect of Oc. But Occitana never came into being and Occitan was supressed altogether.

Golfe
de
Gascogne
Bordeaux
Toulouse
La mer
Mediterranéene
Espagne

Gascony

Today a renewed interest in the old language has filtered into the schools. The old songs are being revived. Young people are studying Occitan in the region's universities.

But for some the old language never really died out. For some, life is just as it always has been in their villages. In the hills, where the farms are isolated, some farmers and their families still speak Occitan at home. Children, albeit rarely, still arrive at school without knowing French. A regular column in the paper still gives the news in Occitan, and entertainment at remote village fêtes may as often as not be in the old tongue.

As a result one may feel that here time has stopped. In the villages, women in black hurry through the streets and disappear down narrow, cobbled alleyways as if fearful, like phantoms, of being exposed to the light. On farms where spring water is heated over a cooking fire in a large, black cauldron to wash the daily dishes in a simple stone sink, a century has passed without perceptively changing anything. One could easily imagine that any tale told here happened yesterday, a generation ago, or even in the last century. Or quite possibly, given the definition of a Gascon, these stories might never have happened at all.

FOR TIM

Esclupé

The region of which I write is poor. It is poor because the land is old and tired and the water scarce. Poverty spawns a curious race of men, when each mouthful is hard-won and everyday necessities are considered luxuries. There are few women, and those who stay are old before their time. One cannot expect generosity from either barren land or a hungry man.

This avaricious climate had created, too, a streak of suspicion and guile which further poisoned the society. If a neighbour did well in some meagre way, all the village looked to see in what way the advantage had been gained at their expense. If a man came to buy a cow, his neighbour mistrusted how he might have come by the money, and at a quick calculation, the means for keeping it. If he could wish bad fortune upon the calving, he did so. If he saw his neighbour's hay go rotten in the swath, he rejoiced. Such was the nature of the people.

And so it is that a simple thing becomes a story. One day a farmer heard that *étrangers*, foreigners, were buying ruined houses to repair as holiday homes. They would pay millions of centimes, some said, for a place in the sunshine.

The farmer was sitting at the café on market day, drinking his third pastis, thinking about this. At last he stood and walked across the square to the office of the *Immobilier*, the estate agent, to present his piece of property for sale.

To him it was but an awkward pile of stones and dangerous timbers in the middle of his field. On top of that, the field was worthless as well. It was bordered by a steep and inaccessible wood which no one had ever tried to cut. As a whole, it seemed a good parcel of rubbish to be rid of. A price was fixed and the old man left the tiny office rubbing his hands with greed.

The piece of property he was selling had come into the hands of his family after the war. The house, garden and woodland stood at the fork of the road which otherwise marked the boundaries of his father's farm. It was for this reason that his father had coveted it. Some said that this was why the old sabotmaker had been reported as a collaborator and shot. His property was naturally enough bought by the neighbour who had, by law, first refusal.

It was called Esclupé or the sabotmaker's house. The new owners took the roof tiles for their own buildings and stored hay beneath a new corrugated iron roof. An old buggy rotted in the undergrowth and a fallen timber trapped the old hay rig. From time to time a shutter moved to speak into the wind, but hidden between the crops, Esclupé was otherwise forgotten.

The sun scorched the earth that summer and animals died of thirst or starvation. The cafés were full of hopelessness and sad tales.

The farmer had been outside when the telephone rang. He had a bell installed so that he could hear it ring if he were in the barn. It took some time to reach it and he wondered crossly if it would stop just as he got to it.

It was the *Immobilier*. There was a client interested in the property. The old farmer put down the phone. It was a difficult instrument to use as he held it some way from his face and shouted towards it. It made it difficult to be certain of what he heard. Esclupé? Would someone really want it after they saw it?

The prospective client arrived with the *Immobilier*, who to everyone's eyes was a thief before he had begun his work. His car was new and clean, his dress casual and expensive, and his scent was not of sweat. Now he conferred with his client in whispers, regarding with contempt the building while extolling the wood, the view and what he termed 'possibilities'.

The Client was a slight, grey-haired man. His healthy body and relaxed attitude spoke of life in a town, not on the land. But it was not this that irritated the Old Farmer, it was his point of view. To the Client, the sun which had impoverished the region was reason enough to buy bad land and buildings not even the Old Farmer would use any more.

And where was this Client from? Germany. Why would he want to have a house in France? It seemed inconceivable to the Old Farmer that anybody should want to go to a country which was not their own. 'Did the Client know this region?' the Old Farmer considered darkly. From another time, perhaps?

The Client's eyes were soft and seemed to be full of love for all they saw. Each piece of disused machinery or ancient tool in the ruins was a marvel to him. He paced out the decayed corpse of the house and reconstructed it mentally. Yes, he would have it.

They would meet at the *Notaire*'s office to sign the agreement to sell and buy. Then there would be a deposit and the Old Farmer would have to match that to change his mind. But would the Old Farmer now agree to sell? He felt that if his price were accepted so easily then surely he had been tricked into pricing it too low. He agreed to sign in two days' time to think it over.

At the café with his neighbours the Old Farmer worried much about the coming contract. Why would anyone pay so much for something worthless?

Some felt that it was the beginning of an influx of foreigners who would take over their region. Others saw it as a developer's trick to build a modern house on the site of the old and then to sell it for triple the price in a year's time to troublemaking French from the cities. Someone felt that it was certainly a hunter who only wanted access to the plentiful hunting afforded to landowners of the *Commune*. Each had a different opinion, until a voice said flatly, 'He knows something.'

Voices dropped and the men drew together.

'He was a simple man, the sabotmaker,' one said.

'He was a collaborator,' spat the Old Farmer. 'Didn't I see with my own eyes the soldier he had in his house?'

They went silent, shaking their heads and reflecting. The memory of the unmarked graves of collaborators in the wood on the hill still haunted some.

'Maybe the German learned a secret,' the first man proposed. 'Does a man die here with no gold in his mattress?'

'Perhaps the soldier gave him money,' another suggested. 'Why else would a man betray his friends and nurse the enemy like that?'

'There was no gold to be found there,' the Old Farmer scoffed. 'He was only a sabotmaker after all.' But doubt had found a foothold.

'The son never returned after the war,' someone reminded them. 'How do you see that? We know he must have died, but perhaps he was murdered so that the soldier could come back one day for the gold.'

'You may be right or you may be crazy,' replied the Old Farmer. 'If you believe your story, why don't you buy the place for the tiny sum I have asked? Then all the gold that you claim is worth murder will be yours.'

They all laughed and someone bought another round of drinks.

'And if I buy it and don't have the secret, how do I profit?' demanded the one, now becoming angry at the turn of the discussion. 'It is your property, you old man, and you should make a search with all your neighbours before you sell that. If there is gold from the Collaborator, it should be divided amongst us all.'

Heads nodded and everyone looked towards the Old Farmer to see how he would take the challenge.

'Never!' he thundered.

'So what will you do then?' demanded a reasonable man with an open-handed gesture.

'We must make a higher bid to see if this Client is serious,' decided another. 'If the Client bids higher, we know that there is more at stake than meets the eye.'

'Who will make a bid then?' asked the Old Farmer, knowing that their words were empty. 'In the end I am left with no money, is that it?'

The Old Farmer dressed in his only suit and the shoes which had been his father's and went to the office of the *Notaire* to sign the contract to sell and buy. They must wait now for three months before signing the final act of sale.

In the afternoons, the Old Farmer was irritated to see the Client walking the country roads past the property, serenely looking about him. The Old Farmer followed his every move with binoculars but without any clues. His very presence, however, gave credence to the myth of the hidden *Louis d'ors*, and soon everyone was whispering of Esclupé.

By night the Old Farmer began his own excavations and by day he patrolled the field. No one could step on this land to search for treasure until the act of sale was signed. Then it would be the Client's problem to guard it. That is, unless the Old Farmer found it first.

However, the offended neighbour exercised his right to pre-empt the sale. The Old Farmer was alarmed to see that he planned to match the price of the Client. This prompted the stubborn Old Farmer to retract his offer of sale, matching the baffled Client's generous deposit in order to take it off the market. The *Notaire* was indignant, the *Immobilier* furious, but the greedy Farmer left the office on a rosy cloud of promised wealth.

It had taken all the money the Old Farmer had and more besides as he had had to sell two of his best cows to manage to get the property back. He would pursue the hidden gold until he died, guarding the ruin with dogs and never speaking to his neighbour again.

And the Client? He sat in the café with the *Immobilier*, who perspired as he spoke in vain of other houses available in the region.

'No,' replied the Client, shaking his head. 'It was only that particular property that interested me. It was the house of my childhood, you see. I was conscripted during the war to work in Germany and while I was gone my father took in and nursed a wounded young German soldier. He told him that it was because he hoped that the others were being kind to his son, too.

'The soldier my father nursed found me and his parents were kind to me. Their son later died, and they shot my father as a collaborator after the war, so you see, it was a logical arrangement for them to adopt me. They said it was just.

'Now I'm getting too sentimental,' he laughed. 'Things haven't changed very much here in all this time. We should never try to go back.'

He paid for the drinks, got into his BMW and drove away. And dust filled the quiet street.

Le Vrai Gascon

From my studio I could look out across an inspiring panorama of nobby hills and ploughed fields that made their way steadily towards the hazy mountains. Tiny corners of red tiled roofs popped up here and there, but other than that there was an eerie sensation that I might be the last person on earth.

In pleasant contrast, on a fine day, not too hot or too cold, I could walk to the little village I knew to be hidden in the next valley with its gregarious population.

Stories rather than gossip surrounded these people like the trappings of theatre, giving rise to an impression that no one used their real names and that the little dramas were all staged for entertainment. There was Agnes-the-widow's-sister and Michel-the-old-carpenter's-nephew. Or more intriguingly, Adele-Marie-the-Italian's-half-sister-because-of-that-business.

Often I took my midday meal at the café, just to watch and listen. They accepted me as if I had always been there at the long table, sharing their cassoulet and wine.

But these people, so I was told and so they hung their heads in admission, were not real Gascons. At the far end of the table a bald and round-faced little man had once called to me that these were all foreigners. Wagging his gnarled finger good-naturedly at them all he told me that they had all come from other places, their children had gone other places. Only he was a true Gascon, of generations of Gascons, guarding their ways and customs. He had never left. The only true Gascon.

And with that, as he was hard of hearing, he retreated into his own pleasant world of his meal, his newspaper and his nap.

It did seem that his special status was respected. Shouting for his attention they would cry, 'Dominique! Dominique! Tell us how much they drank in the old days.' And he would tell them once again how each worker was given his loaf of bread and five litres of wine in a little wicker covered jug from his *patron* before going to the fields.

Or they would tell the old bachelor some shocking tale of some respectable old fellow's infidelity. To which Dominique would give some gem of wisdom such as, '*Oui*, *oui*, when your cow is old you trade her in for a heifer.'

One day Arlette-the-café-owner's-wife placed a plate of langoustines in front of the old man instead of his usual meat course, as a treat. Everyone watched in silence as Dominique carefully attacked the strange creatures.

'They're langoustines,' called a hearty voice. 'Have you ever eaten langoustines, Dominique?'

'*Non*, *non*, we don't have them here.' He shook his head without looking up from his work.

'What do you think of them?' someone asked.

'It's a lot of work for a little piece of meat,' he declared shaking his head gravely.

Dominique wore the *bleu de travail*, the farmer's smock and trousers. He had bought a new suit of it when he had retired from farming his father's twenty hectares. The youngest son, he had stayed at home to look after his parents, using the same tools and wooden-wheeled carts that his father had made from instructions in a farmers' gazette over half a century before.

Now alone, he still worked, mending sacks for the *Coopérative* on his treadle sewing machine. Perhaps his abandonment of all agricultural work on his father's death was the only sign of protest at his empty life of servitude.

From my east-facing window I could see the ridge of his roof, its undulating form suggesting some giant creature crouching in the dell, convinced that if its head were hidden the rest of it would be as well.

This particular roof was often added to a landscape for its colour. Like a crazy-quilt, it bore patches of golden ochre and powder blue lichen, dark and vivid green mosses on its weathered rosy terracotta back.

The house beneath was as simple as its inhabitant. It stood looking squarely before it at what had once been the farmyard, a two-room worker's cottage of typical mud and rubble construction. Sunflowers along the front gave it a welcoming touch.

There were just two rooms: a kitchen and a bedroom. In the first, an enamelled wood-burning cooker dominated the giant fireplace, its flue pipe tipped at an angle up the wide chimney. A few crocks of preserves stood unceremoniously on the mantelshelf. Two chairs sat beside the table which was dominated by an old television set, and a large worn red armchair was pushed near the chimney. From the ceiling a solitary dust-covered bulb hung forlornly.

The bedroom was behind this. It was small and dark, its shutters drawn against the light. On a simple *lit bateau* lay a rolled-up mattress without bedlinen, and on three wall pegs hung Dominique's wardrobe. A large *armoire* held the rest of his possessions.

In cold weather Dominique sat in his Renault 4 with the heater on and the radio for company. On sunny days he could be found on the doorstep between the sunflowers napping. And in his dreams he always smiled.

Such had been and would be his contented life, I sighed to myself. Of course I was mistaken.

One noontime there appeared a woman. Not only from a painter's point of view, she was an arresting sight. Dressed in a simple black shift dress, her grey hair lying in a single plait to her waist, she was the picture of elegance and beauty. Her parchment skin had weathered close to her fine nose and cheek-bones, setting off her enormous black eyes. Her large mouth was merely softened attractively with the tiny lines of time around it, and there hung about her the serenity of age created by experience and not just by years.

From his corner, Dominique slowly raised his head. In his eyes was the look of a young man smitten for the first time by love. And perhaps because they had age in common, the woman sat herself across from him.

I sat back with a smile.

Her name, we learned from eavesdropping on their not-so-private conversation, was Julie. She was from Paris, the widow of a jeweller. She had come on holiday for the *foie gras*, and was impressed by what good value for money Gascony was.

Dominique talked as we had never heard him talk before, and their conversation continued as he escorted her out for a drive in his Renault. This car was reputed never to have been out of second gear so all heads turned as they drove away.

Several days passed before I ate again in the village. Julie was still in town and by now was Dominique's companion at mealtime. She had taken over the conversation, but it didn't seem to matter to Dominique who smiled adoringly at her throughout his meal.

When they left, Arlette-the-café-owner's-wife came over and put a large, dusty bottle on the table and sat down beside me.

'Taste this,' she commanded, pouring some of the amber liquid into the dregs of my coffee.

I held the cup under my nose for a moment and then tasted. A velvet soft Armagnac slid down my throat, caressing with warm fingers as it went.

'Very civilized,' I commented with the raised eyebrow of one who knows the quality they rarely get to taste. The bottle read 'Armagnac' with a date. I gasped.

'Yes,' she agreed peevishly, 'it's nearly 100 years old. Dominique brought it in yesterday and passed it around after lunch. He says he has a cellar full of it.'

'And so?' I asked.

'And so he was succeeded in impressing the Jeweller's Widow,' Arlette declared.

'And is that such a bad thing?' I asked with a little chuckle. 'They seem to enjoy each other's company.'

'Ah, she singled him out immediately,' she smiled wryly. 'All those questions about his property, to a Parisienne it must sound like a fortune: twenty hectares, vineyards, a house and barn, a good pension and all the *foie gras* and Armagnac she cares to consume.

'All she talks about is money. How much things would be worth in Paris. You'd think she had already sold them!'

'But all the same, what does it matter if he is happy?' I reasoned.

'Matter?!' Arlette reproached me. 'It matters to young Paul who is Dominique's cousin's son who will come into the good farmland by the river, and to Hubert and his little wife who hope to buy his house cheap some day so that they can raise a family in a house, not a flat. And it matters to my husband who has promised Dominique his meals for the rest of his days in exchange for that cellar of Armagnac!'

'I see,' I replied nodding thoughtfully. I had forgotten how complex these things could be.

Julie stayed longer than her expected week and speculation on the progress of the romance became the village's main pastime. Stories about when and where the couple had been seen, snippets of their conversations and even a daring peep at a certain postcard bound for Paris were faithfully reported. Could it be that *le Vrai Gascon* would find a mate at last, and from such unlikely a place as Paris?

For my part, my initial sentimentality had begun to fade. As Julie became confident of her conquest, her face hardened and a sharpness, perhaps better described as a condescending impatience, could often be detected in those moments between poses. I became sensitive to her face when she felt unobserved. The flickering distinction between serenity and cold-heartedness fascinated me as an artist, but how I had come to pity Dominique in his folly.

Like most of the village, I agreed that they would no doubt wed, after which she would liquidate her husband's assets. But, I reasoned, if he, were happy at that, what was the real harm? After all, he had always maintained that no one could understand a true Gascon's reasoning, of which I believed simplicity was the key.

However, one day Julie packed her bags and left for Paris without a word. Dominique ate his meal, read his paper and dozed in his corner contentedly as before. Only once when I caught his eye did he seem to acknowledge my unspoken question with a wink.

So he was not so naïve as we had thought. He rose in everyone's estimation, especially when it was revealed that it was she who had paid for his petrol, and after all, her extended stay had been worth quite a bit to the hotel and the café where she had taken nearly all her meals with Dominique.

We raised a glass to him, the clever old Gascon, and the *affaire* ended on a celebratory note.

I had decided to paint the Gascon amidst his sunflowers. When I took the portrait to show him, he began to blush into his radiant smile.

'I wonder what Julie would think of it.' I ventured a leading comment.

'What does it matter?' he shrugged. 'I saw what sort of girl she was, oh *oui, oui.* She asked to see my bedroom,' he confided in a shocked whisper. 'Not a nice girl, oh *non, non, non.*'

I choked back an astonished laugh.

'And besides,' he continued for my instruction, 'in France when a painting is made it is sent directly to the Louvre and there they make picture postcards of it to send all over France. So Julie will surely see it. Everyone will see *Le Vrai Gascon.*'

And with that he smiled, closed his eyes and leaned back against his front door to doze in the sunshine.

Old Uncle

To speak of the old man was to speak of time itself, they said. He could illustrate every event in Gascon history since the Great War with some incident in his long life. They claimed that half the village could rightly call him 'Uncle', and in his own tales he wickedly claimed some closer bonds still, slandering the names of honest grandmothers with the same cold carelessness with which he had seduced them so long ago.

Although he lived in poverty down a medieval alley, he was the proprietor of most of the shops along the single village street. He extracted rents from his young kin without sympathy, disapproving of all equally and begrudging even the smallest repair to the property. As his only comfort was a single electric light bulb, the old miser viewed everything else as extravagance and had the habit of making his observations public.

Old Uncle kept his accounts carefully. Overdue shop rents from his nieces and nephews, forgotten loans to their parents, minute inventories of every chair and coffee bowl that was rightly his, they were all there to be tallied the moment he left this world. As he had no direct heirs, the various relatives assumed that they would divide the Uncle's property by right. After all, he could hardly take it with him. Still the mean old fellow liked to hold this final card as a sort of blackmail, now threatening that everything would be sold upon his death, now taunting that he might legally recognize a son and heir. This became his chief source of amusement in his old age.

Old Uncle called on his relatives at night and without notice, upsetting their meals with his accusations and threats, and driving them to near desperation before relenting and granting them a reprieve just this once. The accusations were usually inventions of his imagination, so there was never a defence. More than one of his own had vowed to do him in and be done with it following one of these fiascos.

On this particular pleasant autumn evening, Old Uncle stopped at the apartment of his eldest nephew, at the nephew's request. This nephew was now in his fifties and had long been running Uncle's own grocery business, living in the rooms over the shop and reporting his accounts to Uncle weekly. He had therefore had the worst abuse from the miserable old man. Why had he actually invited Uncle to see him?

'Uncle, I would like to propose installing a toilet in my apartment,' the nephew announced when curt pleasantries were over. He knew it would mean a fight, but he had carried his tin container of 'night soil' to his allotment for as long as he could remember and he could stand it no longer.

He quickly produced the papers and the plans for the septic tank and drainage, for the plumbing and the beautiful matching wash-basin and shower he planned to install. He would pay for it with his savings, he assured the speechless Uncle, and it would increase the value of the property. How could Uncle refuse such a generous offer as that?

But refuse he certainly did, when he had caught his breath, and let loose a diatribe on the nephew's excesses. If he could save so much as that, then he could afford to pay a higher rent, the old man concluded with venom.

All the reasoning about modern sanitation and all the threats of leaving only made matters worse and in the end, Old Uncle slammed the door on the dreary little flat and stormed downstairs to leave. But there was a thud, a muffled, tumbling sound like a sack of laundry slipping down the stairs, into the back room of the shop below. And then there was silence.

The nephew waited, his heart in his throat for some reassuring sound of the old man getting to his feet. Surely he would be on his stormy way any minute now. But still all was silent.

The nephew opened the door and went cautiously down the stairs as one might approach a wounded fox that might at any moment attack the hand that tried to help it. There was no question about it, Uncle was quite dead. The nephew sat on the stairs, too weak to move. What would they think? Who had heard their argument? They would say he'd pushed his Uncle. And who knew that he had asked him here? What could he do?

'Now, Uncle, there you go. Better?' he said in a loud voice for listening ears. 'You really can't leave like that. Come up and we'll have a drink. Do you remember the time we quarrelled over that woman I was seeing?'

The nephew made the chuckling noises of two men drinking and laughing for some good hour or so, establishing the Uncle's departure as much later than the fall.

'Good-night, Uncle,' he called down the stairs and then shuffled down himself and out the back door in Uncle's jacket and beret. He could see the neighbours in their lighted sitting-rooms from the garden. No one was watching. He crept back into the flat.

Uncle would be found outside the back garden gate. He would appear to have fallen there. He might have been on his way to see the niece who lived next door with some complaint. But he had left his nephew's in good health.

It was not difficult to move Uncle as he was so frail. The body positioned, the nephew hurried to be away. It was a sordid business, he thought.

At eleven o'clock, the garden gate next door opened and the Uncle's niece stepped out to walk her poodle. She never let it foul her garden, leaving it to mess the pavement instead. But on this evening she would change her mind. Opening the gate, she saw an upturned hand on the pavement and to her horror, the body of the Old Uncle lying behind her back wall. The poodle began to growl and bark. Grabbing the little dog, she fled back to the house and her husband.

'What are we to do?' she sobbed. 'It's terrible. Shouldn't we call somebody? The gendarmes, a doctor? My cousin Jerome, he's a doctor…'

'Stupid woman!' hissed her husband. 'Right there behind our garden wall your Uncle, that you've told the world you detest, is mysteriously and conveniently dead. What will they say of that? Why was he here, or what was he coming for? You might have easily dropped a stone over the wall on his head! No, we must move him.'

'But that's horrible! You can't mean that I could be incriminated if he chooses to die near our gate,' she protested, still holding the growling dog.

'And what of the money we owe in back rent?' her husband suggested with meaning. 'And what of Uncle's telling all the café about it? They'll suspect us, certainly. Who else is in trouble with him at the moment? You see what I mean?'

'Yes, yes, I suppose,' she agreed nervously, 'but what are you thinking of doing?'

'Simply to move him from here, far from here,' he replied as he considered. 'We could move him by car to the little park near your cousin Jerome, as if he might have been going to see him. It doesn't make any difference to Uncle where he's found now, anyway.'

The couple crept from the house in darkness, and wrapping Uncle in a blanket, transferred him to the back seat of their shabby 2CV. Without lights, they pushed the car down the street a good distance before starting the engine. They passed the little municipal park with its children's swings and stopped some distance away on the road going out of town. Everything was still.

Making as little noise as possible, even though no houses directly overlooked the park, they placed Uncle beneath a tree, as if he might have fallen and hit his head on a nearby rock. Then they hurried away, the niece looking back over her shoulder as if in fear that he might wake and give chase

In the early hours of the morning, Uncle's nephew, the doctor, and his wife were returning from a concert and evening out in Toulouse. As they turned the corner, their headlamps swept the park.

'Wait!' said the wife. 'I'm sure I saw something in the park. Someone's sleeping out there.'

'Someone waiting to burgle a house in the early hours of the morning, no doubt. I'll call the police when we get home.'

'No, it was a man on the ground,' insisted his wife. 'We must stop to see if he's hurt.'

'Oh, for heaven's sake.' Her husband pulled to a stop crossly. He left the lights on and went to investigate the sleeping man. To his horror, it was Old Uncle, very dead indeed.

'My God, what next?' He sat nervously running his hand through his hair. 'What are people going to say about this? The doctor of the exclusive retirement home leaves his own Uncle to die like a beggar in the park, right on his very doorstep! Just when I could have done without that kind of embarrassment.'

'But he doesn't have to be found here, does he?' his wife looked nervously around them. 'After all, if he were found in a more acceptable place, there would be no scandal. He lived his life as he chose and died happy. He could have been hunting, or fishing, something pleasant.' She shuddered.

'You're brilliant!' her husband replied, jumping from the car. 'Let's get him into the back.'

The doctor reluctantly picked up the dirty old man, thinking what the smell would do to his new wool suit. He opened the boot of his Mercedes as if he were loading a suitcase, closed it and swiftly turned the car.

They headed out into the country. In a quiet valley they stopped to one side of the narrow, pot-holed road and the doctor got out.

'He used to come out this way, walking, to have his wicked way with the old Farmer's Widow,' he chuckled. 'He was always going on that she never turned him down, the old *putain*. We can leave him here as if he just overdid it and fell with a heart attack. Now let's get out of here.'

They drove off, assuring one another that they had done nothing criminal and that nothing could be proved, especially if the doctor himself performed the autopsy.

It was the hour for checking the stock and feeding chickens. The Farmer's Widow and her son were starting their chores. On their isolated farm, one day was much like the next.

The farm was no richer nor poorer than any other scattered amongst the hills. The Widow didn't complain, in fact she never said much at all. She had little company. Still, she had her son.

Her son was a man of nearly fifty, but sadly had been stricken by the fever as a child and so was retarded, forever having the mind of an eight-year-old. He was strong, and willing to do as he was told, and the woman couldn't have asked for a kinder child.

'*Maman*!' the son came across the farmyard calling to her. '*Maman*, it's Old Uncle! He's asleep.' In his arms he carried the filthy, well-travelled Uncle.

His mother ran to see, and then shook her head. 'Take him into the bedroom, son,' she said gently. 'Put him to bed now so that he can sleep.'

She looked at the frail form and contorted face that told of his avaricious and bitter nature and shook her head once more. The Uncle would surely never see heaven. Still, he couldn't die like this.

'Go into the village, son, and find Monsieur the *Curé*. Tell him that he must ring the bell for Uncle, and then come to visit him here,' she instructed as simply as possible so as not to upset the simple man-child.

Alone with Uncle she thought of his cruelty towards her and their son. He had ruined her reputation, lost her the few friends she had had in the village and then taken advantage of her loneliness, using her, promising to legally recognize the boy, and then laughing at her for believing him. But it was over now, and powers greater than she would administer justice to him.

When the *Curé* arrived, Uncle was cleaned and in a fresh shirt to accept the last rites. The Farmer's Widow had seen to it that he should meet his maker with some dignity, even if he had had little in life.

The gendarmes came without ceremony, only eyeing her somewhat curiously, wondering how the notorious Uncle got into her bed. The Old Devil, even at his age!

The Uncle's relatives made appropriate comments, each trying to find some worthy point to make about his life, and professing to have at least tried to be kind to him.

As is customary, the funeral was held immediately as there was no question that his death was natural. The ox-drawn wooden-wheeled hearse made its way slowly up the hill from the church to the graveyard perched at the top.

It was a lonely place. Once the site of an early church, there was no evidence that it had served a community. Its history, like so much of the region's, was lost, burned or obscured in the battles between powerful landlords. Occasionally an old artefact turned up in the gravedigging, and these were placed in the tiny chapel without identification. The present community in the valley below continued to confer their dead to the hilltop as they must have imagined their ancestors had, although that community and church were in fact a comparatively modern establishment.

The road passed around below the graveyard in a semi-circle, a high stone wall fortifying the slope up on one side and a steep drop to the valley on the other. This perilous curve was known as 'Cemetery Bend' and more than a few had thought they would meet their maker there as they met an oncoming vehicle. The tiny party of nieces and nephews, Resistance comrades, and black-shrouded, God-fearing women stopped as the hearse negotiated the tight turning, just as the man they carried might have to do at the Day of Judgement, more than a few were thinking as they watched.

The relatives dressed in black, shared a meal and then went home to wait. The dispersal of an estate takes time. All rubbed their hands in expectation of their just reward for all the years they had suffered Old Uncle's tyranny.

But Old Uncle had not finished with them yet. He had indeed left a will, and its contents were a surprise to everyone.

'My earthly belongings should rightly go to whomever will take me in at the end,' read the *Notaire*, 'for I know that I will have done nothing to deserve their kindness, nor will I have been grateful.'

Uncle may have meant this to be a slightly longer stay with the saintly person he imagined, but the Widow's gesture satisfied the law and could not be matched by any acts of the other relatives, and their protestations about 'that whore' didn't help their case. Uncle was unrepentant to the last.

When the first fine weather came in May, Monsieur the *Curé* went up to the lonely graveyard to clean it up after the long winter. To his surprise and dismay, the road was blocked. The winter rains had saturated the clay, causing the wall to collapse. And there on top of the rubble sat the Old Uncle's coffin.

Some viewed this act of Nature as evidence of some higher opinion as to Uncle's right to be buried with the repentant. Others looked to their own souls, fearing that they, too, might be rejected one day. Whatever the case, the *Curé* was to enjoy a full church for many Sundays to come.

And so it came to be said that in the cemetery of this village there are no ghosts, because the hallowed ground will not let the wicked rest there.

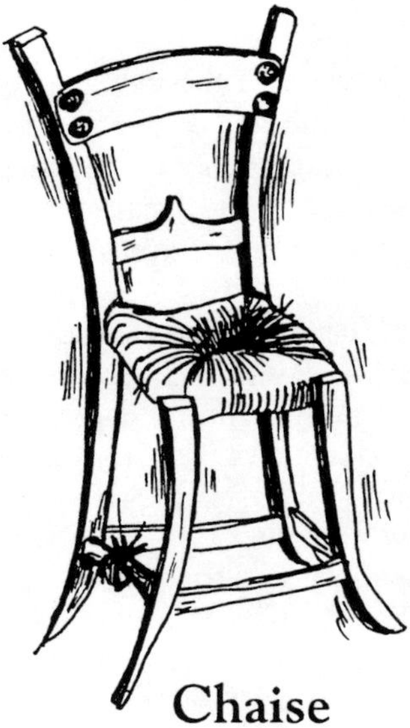

Chaise

French, they will tell you, is the most difficult language in the world. It is so exact that often a paragraph of it is needed to translate a single colourful English word. Or then again, a single French word may represent half a dozen entirely different English ones.

If this is not baffling enough, one finds that the learning of French is almost to the exclusion of learning any other language. The ultimate reasoning is, with a shrug, that their language is the most difficult in the world.

Until the nineteen-forties Gascony was still a bilingual region, with aspirations by some of becoming an independent state of Occitana after The War. That idea being quashed, the promotion of French became an important task. People who went to school in those days now smile at how they were beaten for speaking Occitan, or how one family could feel itself socially superior to their neighbour because only French was spoken in their household.

To an *étranger*, a foreigner, the language barrier in this area then does not imply simply whether or not one can communicate an idea, but rather whether or not the French employed is correct, as language has come to be a mark of social status. Thus even if the regional accent makes '*pain*' into 'pang' and '*champs*' into 'shangs', there is still a high awareness and pride in French. And some are prepared to go to great lengths to explain the subtleties of it to willing, or not so willing, audiences.

The village fair or *fête* in most Gascon communities is an annual affair, a weekend of stalls, perhaps a funfair, and certainly a community meal.

The Committee of Fêtes in this particular village, in this particular year, having decided to further themselves politically, had invited the Regional Councillor in the hope that a grant might follow for a renovation of their village hall.

The existing hall, or *Salle des Fêtes*, was a less than festive edifice, badly in need of paint and lacking windows which gave it the distinct air of being a storage facility for the nearby agricultural depot. On an ordinary, sultry summer evening, the mingled smells of pastis and Gauloise cigarette smoke were strong enough to preserve hams in the rafters. Something had to be done, and preferably with government money.

So, to further the warm impression that a good country meal was bound to make, the Committee had decided to include a demonstration of arts and crafts, as the neighbouring village had done the year before. That fortunate place had been written up in all the papers, and the Councillor himself had spoken at great lengths on the virtues of preserving the old traditions and crafts as an important part of the region's cultural heritage.

The Committee of middle-aged businessmen shook their grey heads at this. They had fought all their political lives to drag their village out of just such backward ways and practices, had stood firmly against encouraging 'marginals' and foreigners installing themselves in the hills to scrape their living from inefficient and embarrassingly primitive occupations, and were now simply bewildered at the current fads. But politics being politics, they had put out a call for artisans.

One of these artisans was a young immigrant. Her craft was spinning, and if she spoke little French it hardly mattered for the demonstration. Artisans, it turned out, were not so easy to come by.

On the morning of the fair, the *Fileuse* brought her spinning wheel and fleeces to spin for the public. She hung samples of spun yarn and weavings to create an interesting backdrop, lay sacking on the ground to keep the wool clean and found a level spot for her wheel.

With her she also brought a pretty little spindled chair. At home it was only decorative because it was not only weak in its elderly joints, but a brace was cracked at the bottom as well. Today, however, she wanted everything to look right, and the chair nearly matched her wheel. If she sat carefully, it would hold her weight, she decided.

She unpacked the clean, teased wool that she had prepared for spinning and began gently pumping the treadle of her wheel. People paused and stopped, some smiled and spoke. The time passed as the fibres slipped through her skilful fingers and magically filled the bobbin with yarn.

At noon, all the artisans were invited to eat as guests of the Committee. The tables set out in the square were planks on trestles, covered with paper cloths which seemed determined to escape before any dishes arrived to weight them down. The atmosphere was chaotic as villagers and visitors flocked into the square, squeezing together on to benches made of straw bales, and jumping up to catch the fluttering paper tablecloths with hoots of laughter.

The Committee were looking concerned at the unexpectedly large turnout for the meal. The Councillor had not yet arrived and space on the crowded benches was nearly filled, even at the Mayor's table.

The Councillor was as large as he was important and it was decided that the problem would be most easily solved by finding a chair for the big man and seating him at the head of the table. A Committee member ran off to borrow one from the café.

But the café was some distance away and the day was warm. On the way the man spotted the vacant chair of the *Fileuse*. What a stroke of luck. No one would need it during the meal. He was back with it in but a moment, just in time to put it in place before the honoured man arrived.

The tables were buzzing with the foreign words that left the poor *Fileuse* feeling dizzy and confused. She would smile and try to respond to simple questions, but people soon lost patience with her awkward French and found other companions. She looked about her for signs of food but was frozen by what she saw at the head table. The *Fileuse* couldn't believe her eyes. Surely it was simply a coincidence that the men had found a chair like hers. Still, she left her place and ran to be sure. It was indeed her little chair that was about to take the weight of the great and mighty man.

She caught the arm of a Committee member who had just arrived with baskets of bread. He frowned at being stopped.

'My seat,' she whispered in excitement, pointing towards the head table.

' "Seat" is masculine.' The man corrected the personal pronoun patiently. ' "*Le siège*." Now excuse me.' He turned to be about his serving, but she tried again to explain, cursing her ignorance of French.

'No,' she said taking a breath to steady herself. 'My seat is stolen,' she said, pointing to the Councillor who was already helping himself to bread and wine. Excitedly she added, 'There!'

'Ah, you mean "chair" ', the man exclaimed, understanding at last. 'It is a chair, "*une chaise*", chair is feminine.

"You see, a "seat" is used as in a political or judicial seat, or in a grander sense, a central or head office. Sometimes it is also used in the sense of a location, such as the seat of an illness or the seat of the problem.

'You, however, mean a simple chair, as in a baby's chair or a deck-chair,' he smiled now, putting down the bread and warming to his subject.

'As for "stolen", "*volée*", this is most interesting. Although I take your meaning, it can also mean "flown" in which case you have used very beautiful French indeed to say that your chair has flown. But I fear you're not so advanced as yet.

'The word you probably wanted was "taken", from the verb "*prendre*". It can also mean to bring, or to pick up or to put on, as with your glasses, or to get or to fetch... You really should study that one as it can be a very handy verb for the everyday life.

'On the other hand, you should say that the chair has been borrowed, because they are going to return it to you. "*Emprunter*", "to borrow". And then you would also say that you have lent it. "*Prêter*", "to lend". This can sometimes mean that you claim something, as you said at first, you "lent them the intention of stealing your chair!" ' He smiled broadly at his clever turn of phrase.

'The chair's broken!' she sobbed, now full of frustration and anxiety. 'Get it back!'

'Now that is a complicated one,' he continued. 'You used "*brisé*", meaning rightly enough "broken", but that is used more in the sense of ruined or wrecked, although you could mean "exhausted",' he suggested helpfully.

' "*Rompre*" also means "to break" but that is more commonly used in association with human affairs, as in breaking a commitment or a bad habit.

'Now you see why French is the most difficult language in the world?' he interjected enthusiastically. 'All the subtleties to learn. I still read a book with a dictionary close at hand so that I can check to see in what sense an author might be using a word.

'But the word you want in this case must be "*casser*", "to break" in the sense of crack and snap," he concluded with a satisfied smile.

But she grabbed his arm and pointed vigorously toward the head table, 'Say "*chaise cassé*", quick!' she cried.

But it was too late. The '*gros legume*', the 'fat vegetable', as they poetically choose to call the bigwigs, was laughing and rocking back on two legs of the little chair. Holding his glass of wine high as if announcing the whole little tragedy, he disappeared with a sound of cracking and snapping wood. '*Casser*' was indeed the correct word.

The Mayor and the Committee rushed to rescue the heavy Councillor. 'No grant for the village hall,' they all were thinking as they fussed and brushed and fawned.

From where the *Fileuse* stood, it was a perfect farce. The men fell over one another, trying each to be the one to pull the Councillor to his feet from behind the table. The paper tablecloth began to blow away, but not before it had lain across a lighted cigarette in a nearby ashtray and begun to burn merrily in the wind. A helpful Committee member threw a glass of wine to put it out, also hitting the shirt of his colleague and thus starting an argument. The Councillor rose like a grand elephant from below, but in doing so knocked one of the planks of the makeshift table off the trestles, sending bread, wine and burning cloth to the ground. From somewhere a siren whined and there came the sound of 'pam pom, pam pom', as if the *pompiers*, the fire brigade, might be preparing to join the mayhem.

The *Fileuse* began to laugh. It was a sweet, bell-like sound that was infectious. The Committee man beside her covered his growing smile with his hand as he began to chuckle. They were joined quickly by everyone in the crowd. It was a common language, and it said it all.

Madame of the Auberge

The *tue-cochon*, the pig kill, had begun at the *Auberge*. Ropes swung from the rafters of the open-sided barn where the butcher and some twenty-odd guests awaited the procession. Knives and saws lay on a freshly scrubbed table, a wooden trough on the ground near by. Buckets of water boiled over a brazier. Soon a dirty, terrified beast would be tamed into docile hams and sausages before everyone's eyes.

The fattened pig began to squeal as soon as the men entered the dark, cool shed. Shouting, they prodded and bullied him into the November sunshine, into the poke which would carry him to his death. There was only a slight chill to the wind which carried his shrill cries over the rolling hills of the Gascon countryside.

The guests watched in fascinated horror as the Butcher expertly trussed the pig's hind legs and a team of men hoisted the doomed animal so that he hung well off the ground. The noise of his cries were now deafening and the faint-hearted turned away. With practised skill the Butcher plunged his knife deep into the exposed throat and slit it neatly.

'I'm pregnant,' a tense voice whispered into a certain ear.

Monsieur of the *Auberge* felt suddenly ill as he watched the pig's blood fill the waiting basin. He could see himself hanging in its place, feet trussed, as the Butcher slit his throat.

'But he can't prove anything, Elaine,' Monsieur whispered reassuringly. 'It could be his own, after all.'

'You know very well he will know that it is not his,' she replied angrily in a hiss. 'It is nearly a year since I have slept with him!'

'Calm, calm,' Monsieur soothed. 'Then you may well have to kiss and make up.'

'We must talk later,' she said and moved away as her husband looked up from his bloody work.

Monsieur of the *Auberge* was shaken, but sensibly reminded himself that it was unlikely that the Butcher would find them out if Elaine could be persuaded to take her jealous husband back into her bed. There was no need to panic.

Unfortunately, the couple's hushed words behind the house had drifted upward and through a tiny bathroom window, transfixing an eavesdropper within.

The village seamstress arranged herself and prepared to return to the company below. An idea had already begun to form and she smiled to herself.

The Seamstress was thin and elegant, with sharp features and fussy, nervous habits. Aristocratic by birth, she had never been able to accept her life as an impoverished widow. She had been reduced, she would complain, to the *couturière*'s trade. Or as most people saw it, she had to work as everyone else did.

Generally speaking, the Seamstress was as unpopular a person as could be found in the village, yet Madame of the *Auberge* never failed to invite her to events such as this. After all, the Seamstress had rich and powerful relations and one must use one's head in a business such as hers.

So it was to oil the wheels of business that the Seamstress had been invited, and it was for a free meal that she had accepted.

The pig was now cut in half, hinged as it were by the thick skin of its back. Its organs lay in various containers awaiting attention. The men had scraped the hair from the skin as the carcass was scalded in the wooden trough. The Butcher now worked both hands through the blood which would be used in the casings for the *boudin noir*. The guests sipped pastis or wine as they admired the morbid display.

The Butcher was strong and lean, handsome in the dark Gascon way. His skill was such with a knife, they said, that he could halve a fly without appearing to have done so. He was equally renowned for his jealousy regarding his beautiful if faithless wife and his temper.

'It would be terrible to think what that man could do if he were angry,' the Seamstress remarked to Monsieur of the *Auberge* as he was gazing absently at the hanging pig.

'Not a pleasant thought,' he replied almost to himself.

'I wonder if he could be held responsible for his actions if, for instance, he were to discover not only the name of his wife's lover but also that she is carrying that man's child,' she said with meaning.

The blow struck. Monsieur turned slowly with a look of total disbelief. The Seamstress directed his gaze with her eyes towards the little window of the bathroom. He winced slightly.

'What do you want?' he asked with resignation.

'These things are things of business,' she said briskly. 'Two thousand francs each month until the child is born and then we are finished and I forget.'

'As soon as I can,' he groaned.

'By Monday morning,' she corrected. 'I will buy meat at eleven o'clock.'

He sighed and nodded. He was after all a rich man.

'Dear Madame!' came the cry from a large, effusive woman with hair the unfortunate colour of wine stain. 'I have been searching for you everywhere.'

The Seamstress advanced with some dignity, kissing her hostess on both cheeks. Madame of the *Auberge* was a woman 'of a certain age' as they say, although her bright eyes and inexhaustible enthusiasm gave her an air of youth. Now she slipped an arm through that of the Seamstress and led her away and into the house.

'I must speak with you,' she whispered with an air of girlish secrecy. They mounted the stairs to Madame's bedroom suite and office.

'You see,' she explained as she began hunting through a drawer in her wardrobe, 'the New Year's festivities will be very special to us this year. It is the twenty-fifth anniversary of our first meeting and I want my husband to be reminded of our romance once again. I know, you will say, "What an old fool she is to be so sentimental," but that is how I am.

'What I want is a gown which will flatter me, something of style and the best *tissu*. I would like you to go to Paris to see the latest styles and to buy the fabric. Here, take this and spare no expense.'

With that Madame of the *Auberge* took out a box containing a disorderly stack of banknotes of various denominations. Trembling with excitement, she took the money and pressed it into the Seamstress's hands, dropping several bills as she did so.

'I am so happy about this,' she beamed. 'I know that you will make me look wonderful.'

In fact Madame's motive was also to ally herself with the Seamstress's relations in Paris, where she would certainly stay. Their custom would come to her when they returned the visit, certainly buying cases of her *foie gras* and *confits*.

The rest of the party was a huge success as Madame's good humour was contagious. They ate the traditional meal of the *tue-cochon*, beginning with a chicken broth and fried pig's throat, then following with four other courses of meats, none being pork. Wine flowed, and spilled, and the company relaxed into bad jokes and ribaldry.

That night in her cold, narrow bed the Seamstress felt, as it were, twice blessed. She anticipated paying the grocer, ordering fuel for the winter and travelling to Paris with equal pleasure as she drifted to sleep still clutching her new fortune under her pillow.

The following morning she walked briskly down the village street to purchase fresh croissants to eat with her coffee.

'Have you heard?' asked Madame of the *Boulangerie* in the whisper reserved for death. 'Madame of the *Auberge* is dead! Murdered, they say and robbed.

'How dreadful!' murmured the Seamstress, feeling weak with creeping horror.

'Murdered after her party,' the *Boulangère* added with finality as if all the world might expect the same fate after such an event.

The Seamstress bought her rolls and walked slowly towards her little apartment. Now here was a dilemma: Madame had given her cash in secret. This was perhaps the money that was thought to be stolen as she had given nearly every bit in her box. Should the Seamstress begin spending large sums of money now, she would surely become the first suspect in the murder. So too would she be suspected if she spent the money she was going to extract from Monsieur on Monday in blackmail. She must go at once to the police, return the money and explain the situation.

At the *Auberge* she found the gendarmes methodically searching the garden and lawns around the house. Gathering her courage, she marched to the front door and asked to speak with the head of the investigation.

She was shown to the front parlour where Monsieur was just saying goodbye to Monsieur the *Curé*. Faces were solemn and voices hushed. The room smelled musty with the first dampness of the winter.

After exchanging a few polite words with her, the *Curé* said good-day and left the Seamstress facing Monsieur of the *Auberge* alone.

'What are you doing here?' he asked between clenched teeth.

'I have evidence to give,' she replied coldly. 'Your poor wife was not robbed.'

'And I suppose that you know what happened to the money?'

She held the notes for him to see.

'I was to make a dress for her. She wanted me to go to Paris for the pattern and cloth,' she explained.

'You are indeed an admirable fool,' he laughed coldly. 'You have no proof that you had any dealings with my wife which could have involved so great a sum of money. I think it is more likely that you are the shrewd, desperate woman who would stoop to blackmail, and that makes you an equally likely suspect for murder.'

His face began to harden as she visibly lost her confidence. She had misjudged him.

'A dress,' he said with scorn. 'She said she had spent the money on a dress! I had crept into her room, to her money box, when I thought she was saying goodbye to the last of the guests, but the box was open and empty. Then she walked in, telling me the money was gone to buy a dress. What did she care how it was for me to find your ransom. I could die by the Butcher's knife, but she would have a new dress!'

'But blackmail is a common thing,' she reminded him. 'You did not complain because we both know that you are rich enough to afford to guard your secret. Murder is much different.'

He turned away, his shoulders slumped.

'I hit her,' he said simply. 'I only felt surprise as she fell. She didn't get up. I sat there all night. I just couldn't believe she was dead.'

The approaching fall of disciplined bootsteps made them both turn towards the door. Steps rang on the tiles then stopped only long enough to rap once before the Captain entered the room.

The Captain was a distinguished man in his mid-fifties, with an enormous curving moustache. Now the ends of it twitched, showing the only signs of surprise at what he saw before him. The Seamstress was kissing Monsieur fully on the mouth while banknotes lay around them on the floor.

Monsieur struggled to free himself, as the wily Seamstress turned to the Captain with stage tears in her eyes.

'Captain,' she sobbed, 'I couldn't keep his blood-stained money. If only things could have been different. He was so good to me.'

She sank dramatically to the couch with the assistance of the bewildered Captain. He handed her his handkerchief gallantly.

As the assisting officers escorted the dumbfounded Monsieur of the *Auberge* out of the house, she cried plaintively, 'Hubert, I'll wait for you, *mon cher*!'

The Captain tactfully suggested that now that the whereabouts of the missing money were known, and Monsieur in custody, it might be better if she kept it to get her through these difficult times. After all, a man had a responsibility to his mistress.

The charge against Monsieur was quickly reduced to that of a crime of passion. He realized that by not denying the story of the Seamstress, he freed himself not only from her blackmail but from the Butcher's knife as well.

The Butcher's wife was quick to put things to rights in her bedroom when she saw how things had turned. The baby would please her husband so much that he would never notice that it came a few months earlier than expected.

And the Seamstress? Her standing in the village increased substantially upon the revelation of such a well-concealed affair, and many were disposed to doing her small kindness while her lover was in prison. After all, one day she might become the new Madame of the *Auberge*.

The Table

In a cramped apartment over a tiny bicycle shop, Mme Begnet sat with her accounts. The summer heat was stifling but she did not open the windows. The city air was too full of dirt and dust and probably hotter than the air in the darkened room. The windows periodically rattled and the floor shook as heavy vehicles passed close to the blackened brick buildings along the narrow Toulousean street.

Mme Begnet was seated at a long table which ran the length of the room. It was a handsome table, made of golden oak and having six finely turned legs. It could easily seat twelve people, although the Begnets seldom had guests and when they did, there were only four chairs on which to sit anyway.

The table instead served as the Begnets' office on one end and the centre for Madame's sewing on the other. The couple dined on a little table in the kitchen.

Although the table was a valuable object, the Begnets never thought of it as such. They never intended to sell it as it was so useful and besides, it had always been in the family.

On this particular afternoon Mme Begnet was feeling cross with the heat. She was tired of being confined to an upstairs apartment in a dirty city where not even a window-box could survive. She hated the noise and resented the high commercial *charges* they paid for this 'prime location'.

It grew all afternoon, this feeling of discontent. And so when her husband finally closed the shop and came upstairs, she exploded as women do, with words and tears and flailing arms.

And her husband quite agreed with her.

So it was in this way that the Begnets came to buy a shop in a quiet Gascon village.

People of the village, however, were quite surprised. Who would leave the exciting life of the city for a poor, sleepy little village? What kind of a living could anyone make in a bicycle shop in an area where everyone could fix their own? They must be either rich or crazy.

The villagers watched, therefore, with great curiosity as the van labelled '*déménagements*' stopped outside the vacant shop. Madame of the *Epicerie* pushed her son outdoors to help the new people and to report what he saw.

The trappings of the business came first: bicycles old and new, spare parts and tools. The work-bench and counter were a struggle; a few boxes and armchairs came out easily. Then looking back into the van the boy saw the table. The question was answered, they were rich.

'I'll get some men to help,' the boy called as he raced down the street, first to his mother and then to the café across the street.

'You must eat with us.' Mme *Epicerie* came down the street smiling broadly. 'It is the hour. The rest can wait.'

The Begnets gratefully accepted her invitation. The meal was leisurely and a full five courses. They sat in a cool dining-room with a red tiled floor, the doors opening to a terrace and garden which Mme Begnet greatly admired.

As the meal progressed neighbours and relatives stopped in and joined them at whatever course was being served until the party had swelled to twelve. Four of the male guests offered to help with the table after lunch, to the relief of the Begnets. Monsieur of the *Epicerie* was an excellent host and kept the glasses full. Conversation grew more animated as each of the volunteers boasted of his past experience at moving furniture.

If was nearly half-past three when the company parted, thanking the family of the *Epicerie*, and the volunteers confronted the table. Mme Begnet had forgotten how beautiful it was, how rich its golden colour, with all those years it had been covered with papers and sewing. Never again, she thought.

It was a fine piece of furniture, everyone agreed. The four volunteers solemnly lifted it down from the van and began its ceremonial journey through the shop to the back stairway which led to the apartments upstairs.

This stairway went up to a landing then turned and went up again at a ninety degree angle to the first floor. The group stopped at the foot of it and considered.

Monsieur the *Menuisier* took charge of the manoeuvres up the stairway as he claimed to have had the most experience in turning large pieces of furniture. Directing that the table be carried on its side, he led them boldly upward. At the turn, the first half of it got around but there the party halted as the middle legs caught with a crack against the protruding corner.

'Stop! stop!' cried the *Menuisier*. 'Take it back down. Those middle legs will have to come off.'

Too late. As they struggled to back the table around the corner everyone could see that one of the legs had split. The table was laid carefully upside down on the shop floor.

'Never mind the little split,' he reassured the Begnets. 'We have an excellent *ébéniste* who does wonders with broken furniture. Now we will just unscrew these screws to take off these middle legs.'

The screws refused to budge and kept their teeth fastened tightly in the joints.

'Never mind,' said Monsieur the *Pharmacien*, who was never a patient man. 'There is so much woodworm in the middle brace that it should be taken off and treated anyway. When it is off, we can chisel the legs off. There is no difference if Monsieur the *Ebéniste* must fix the split leg anyway.'

The Begnets stood by helplessly as the well-meaning band of volunteers set to with all manner of chisels and hammers. Finally brace and legs were removed with much splintering of wood.

Once more the men and the table began to climb the stairs. The turn was a tight squeeze but they made it. The Begnets heard them cheer as they disappeared from view.

Then came a mighty thud followed by a scraping noise and then a squeak of wood against wall. The line of the stairs and the doorway met the inside corridor perpendicularly and the table was now wedged in the turning. The *Menuisier* was beside himself, shouting, 'Back! back! stop!

Non, non, merd alors! Putain de...'

Back in the shop, the table lay on its back like a dead animal, its legs stiff in the air.

'We must think,' the *Pharmacien* said scratching his chin.

'I have it!' cried Monsieur the *Boulanger*. 'Remember the grand *armoire* my wife inherited and how we got it upstairs through the window?'

'Ah oui!' the volunteers cried in unison.

'Don't worry,' the *Boulanger* assured the Begnets. 'This is a very good idea.'

The necessary equipment was fetched for the operation and the table was righted again. Jute sacks, a ladder and a long length of heavy rope lay outside by the door. The Begnets looked at each other and waited to see what would happen next.

The *Menuisier* went up the ladder with the sacks and placed them carefully on the ridge of the roof. Then he returned for the rope, half of which he lobbed over to the back of the narrow house and half he let hang to the front.

In the meantime, Monsieur from the *Quanquierie* and Monsieur the *Boulanger* had opened the door into the back garden so that they could now be seen from the open shop front, making preparations at the rear.

The *Pharmacien* had already opened the large window at the front on the first floor and called that it was just wide enough. Below, the *Menuisier* was securing the rope around the centre of the table. He instructed M. and Mme Begnet to go upstairs to let them know when it was in position to pull in, and sent the *Pharmacien* to go and assist the others in the garden. He himself would direct this triumph.

The table rose slowly with much shouting from everyone to each other to 'watch out' and 'be careful' and 'slowly, slowly'. It came into view and inched slowly past the window ledge with the aid of M. Begnet until it was directly opposite the opening.

'Secure it there,' called M. Begnet excitedly.

The order was repeated in military fashion. The men in the garden secured the rope to the iron railing by the rear door and started up the stairs to pull the table inside.

Suddenly there were noises, serious noises. The old railing creaked, then tore free, flying up and breaking into an upstairs window. The table dropped out of sight before the Begnets' eyes. But there was no immediate crash. The railing and an attached piece of reinforced cement had caught in the top corner of the window.

Below, the *Menuisier* had been on his way to join the men on the stairs. Now he rushed to the front door, expecting to find the table in pieces in the street, but it was nowhere to be seen. He slowly looked up. There hung the table in eerie silence. Then came a sound from the roof, a slow splintering noise followed by a sudden 'Crack!' The table dropped a foot, then jerked as a man at the gallows. There it broke neatly in half at the unsupported middle and fell in earnest, breaking the large glass shop window with a leg as it passed.

The noise above was the main roof beam giving way under the shock and stress of the manoeuvre.

But now the iron railing and attached cement, no longer held by the weight of the table on the other side, dropped from the demolished window to the step at the back door, throwing a lump of detached cement through the back door window almost as an afterthought of Fate.

The Begnets crept cautiously down the stairs, prepared for the roof to fall in at any moment. They surveyed the broken windows, the sagging roof and the pile of wood that had until two hours ago been their table. Mme Begnet broke down into tears.

'Madame, Madame, do not despair,' Monsieur from the *Quanquierie* urged. 'Is this not really a blessing in disguise?'

She looked up at him in disbelief.

'Think now. Your lovely table must have a suitable place. Look behind you. Is that not where it should be?' He gestured grandly and they all turned around to look into the shop.

Catching the idea, the *Menuisier* continued, 'Yes, yes, I see it! The table will be here on the ground floor, with the doors that open to the garden, just as you so admired this noon. It would take but a few bricks to close this opening — which you would have to fix anyway — to make a front door and window of your house.'

He smiled convincingly as Mme Begnet tried to imagine the room from the shambles before her.

'A few tiles and some paper on the walls and *voilà*!' he finished.

'And think, too,' added Monsieur the *Boulanger*, 'if you hadn't discovered that roof beam was weak, it might have collapsed in a storm. This way it can be braced and mended before you move in. And all on the insurance as well.'

M. Begnet brightened at this. But then he frowned, 'What about my shop?'

'Ah, Monsieur, it happens that today is truly your lucky day,' replied

Monsieur of the *Quanquierie*. 'See here, next door? This little shop is empty and I happen to own it. So, I can rent it to you very cheaply indeed. It is not as big as the other, but you can use the garage behind for your work for no extra charge.'

The men promised to arrange for the Begnets to meet some local builders and took the pieces of the table to the *Ebéniste* in the *Menuisier*'s little van that very afternoon.

There was a family hotel in the village, ordinary but with good food, as the Begnets would have to find other accommodation until at least part of the work was finished on their house. The Begnets retired to the hotel, exhausted but happy to have moved to such a friendly, helpful village.

And in the café the villagers were drinking the health of their new neighbours and congratulating themselves on their good fortune at having people with such a table move into their village.

Mamie's Miracle

Mamie sat in her usual seat outside the front door. From beneath her bell-shaped straw hat she sullenly watched the passing traffic. Two cars had passed so far that morning. A neighbour's children sailed by on bicycles.

'I should jump up and frighten them,' she thought bad temperedly. 'They think I'm dead, or why didn't they say, "*bonjour*"?'

A woman of roughly fifty hurried around the house and splashed water on the pots of geraniums by the fence at the roadside. They would bloom soon, Mamie noticed.

The woman was her daughter-in-law, a harassed, brusque sort that believed in getting on with things, as she put it. She was dressed in her husband's clothes as their budget couldn't afford such nonsense as two sets of work clothes. She lived for the farm and their children, as did her husband, and neither ever complained of personal want.

'I'm thirsty,' whined Mamie as she eyed her daughter-in-law from under her hat.

'You would be,' replied the other woman, though not in an unkind tone. 'It's coming.'

She returned in an instant with a cold lemon drink and deposited it without ceremony on the table beside Mamie and disappeared once more.

Mamie put the drink to her lips. She preferred a straw. The mix was watery, she noticed, not enough syrup again. She stretched her black-stockinged legs. They were stiff. She regarded her bedroom slippers, her *pantoufles*, for a moment. She finished the lemon drink and smoothed her blue-flowered pinafore. Beneath it she wore a simple black dress, one of the two which comprised her wardrobe. She leant forward and peered up the road. The postman would be coming soon.

'Marie!' Mamie called as she heard the noises of lunch being prepared in the kitchen. 'Have you fed the poultry?'

'Yes, Mamie,' came the reply.

'Marie, are you making lunch?' Mamie asked, knowing that she was.

'Yes, Mamie,' said Marie, coming to the door. She was Mamie's granddaughter-in-law and did most of the household chores. These had been Mamie's tasks until she had had a mild heart attack, so she felt obliged to make sure that the younger girl was doing things as she should.

'Did you want anything?' the girl asked, slightly exasperated.

'No,' replied Mamie sullenly to this. She eyed Marie's big stomach. They couldn't afford another baby. They had one to look after as it was. Mamie didn't like children, they were always running about and getting into things when you weren't looking.

The postman stopped, got out of his yellow van, came through the gate and up the walk to where Mamie sat. 'Bills and advertising,' she thought.

'How are you feeling today, Madame?' he asked in the booming voice he used for the elderly.

'I'm feeling old!' she retorted. 'And I've got a weak heart, not bad ears!'

He smiled pleasantly and handed her the post, wishing her a good day. 'They are all like that around here,' he thought dismally to himself.

Mamie thumbed through the post and stopped abruptly. There was a picture postcard of little St Bernadette of Lourdes. It was addressed to her.

'Marie!' Mamie called. 'Bring me my spectacles. I have received a picture postcard!'

It might even be said that Mamie was happy for a moment over this small and unexpected thoughtfulness, however, as she read the card, her face resumed its scowl.

'The old hypocrite!' she cried, flinging down the card. Marie picked it up and read, 'My beloved family has sent me on a pilgrimage to Lourdes in the hope of restoring my health. Heaven be praised! You will be in my prayers. Julianna.'

Mamie eyed Marie as she read, 'That woman is only boasting that her family has the money for her to take a holiday, you know,' she said peevishly. 'And it's a fact that her family despises her and she them. Everyone knows it. I hope she sent the whole *Commune* cards so they can all see how she is. Prayers? I doubt whether she could remember the "Our Father" it's been so long since she went to Mass. Some people!' she finished, her black Gascon eyes flashing.

The postcard was given a place on the mantelshelf beside the pots of strawberry preserves and *confits*. Mamie could eye it as she sat silently at the table over her soup. She would mutter, 'Pilgrimage! Bah!' or 'Her health!' with disgust.

For five days Mamie brooded over the picture postcard. Julianna was a friend from childhood. They had grown up in the same *Commune* and had had their first communion together. Thus it was only natural that they should have remained the worst of rivals and the bitterest of undeclared enemies. The fortunes of their neighbouring farms, the accomplishments of their children, even the flowers displayed in their front gardens were matters for competition. This last, however, had seemed to be a challenge of a different sort. It involved religion.

A trip to Lourdes was not a long journey nor an impossibly expensive one. It was simply a blatant extravagance when most farms — hard working, honest folks' farms, Mamie thought to herself — had more important uses for the money.

Then again, this challenge did concern the honour of their farm. Could Mamie sit by and let it be said that her own family would not do as much for her? It would surely be noted by every neighbour in the *Commune*.

Mamie thought of the roll of money which she guarded, stitched up in her mattress. She could well afford to make a pilgrimage and send cards just as Julianna had done. After all, Julianna might have just as well financed her own trip in the same way, if the truth were known.

'I think,' Mamie began one noontime at the table, 'I'm going on a pilgrimage to Lourdes.'

Her son, Jacques, stopped eating with a fork full of noodles half-way to his open mouth. Henri and Louis, his grown sons looked in amazement from their father to their mother, waiting for someone to say something.

The baby, crawling about under the table, sensed some impending row, ran to his mother and began to cry. Claire, the daughter-in-law, obviously felt this would call for a lengthy discussion and returned the plate of meat she was carrying to the kitchen. It was Marie who spoke at last.

'But how can you travel, Mamie? You're not well.' She soothed the fretful toddler while the child eyed Mamie suspiciously. She had a nasty habit of cuffing him when no one was looking.

'Exactly,' Mamie nodded. 'That's it exactly. I'll go in hope of a miracle to cure me as my dear friend Julianna has done. A coach leaves once a month from the village, and they look after you very well. It will be quite all right. After all, a great number of invalids travel to Lourdes.'

There was surprisingly little discussion. What could be said? All the family escorted Mamie to the coach on the day of departure. It was parked just outside the church, allowing the passengers a moment of reflection before the departure.

Mamie kept up a pious expression, clutching her rosary as she was helped aboard the coach. She said that she would keep them in her prayers, as that was what people seemed to be saying. The family looked solemn and worried as they waved her off into the distance.

Now came an exhilarating feeling of devilment as Mamie realized that she was on her way. Julianna would have to dream up something better than this to get the better of her old rival.

The trip took nearly four hours with a satisfactory number of stops. Most of Mamie's companions were elderly, some absorbed in prayer and some simply staring vacantly out of the windows. The coach was stuffy as the sun grew hotter. The travellers became silent as they approached their destination.

The Pyrenees came into view on the left, a panoramic view of snow-capped peaks rising behind the rolling farmland. It was just as if someone had placed a picture postcard behind an ordinary scene, thought Mamie. They had no view of the mountains at home. She longed to open the windows as they must surely get a cool breeze off the mountains, but it was forbidden with respect to the other passengers.

At the terminus, white-coated volunteers advanced with wheelchairs as coaches arrived. Mamie allowed herself to be helped out of the coach and into a waiting chair, pushed by a pretty and smiling young woman. Most of her party, however, continued on foot.

Mamie was enjoying herself. Julianna probably hadn't had a wheelchair and attendant, she thought.

The souvenir shops rolled past. Blue plastic bottles in the shape of the Virgin Mary to hold holy water from the *source*, plastic plaques reading 'Souvenir of Lourdes', cards of a smiling Pope, it was dazzling. Yes, she would like to buy some cards. She wondered whether anyone might take her picture.

Mamie had sunk low in the chair so that her bell-shaped straw hat seemed to sit directly upon the shoulders of her high-collared black dress. She began to feel bewildered as the crowd moved about her. Looking up to get a better view of her fellow pilgrims, she saw a woman with no arms beside her and quickly looked away. A spastic teenaged boy struggled along, supported by an attendant, and a group of blind people, their white canes tapping, followed a robed priest. A line of severely disabled and deformed children sat in a row of miniature wheelchairs, waiting for their attendants to buy them postcards.

All around her the pious and the pitiful were surging forward. Did they really believe that something would happen? Did people really believe in miracles? Or were they, like Mamie, there not to be outdone, to spite their only friend? She had the guilty feeling that it was the former.

And if a miracle happened today, at any moment in the *Grotte*, would all the poor invalids who believed get out of their wheelchairs? Or would only one worthy person be chosen? And why would they be chosen, and would everyone who witnessed it be able to hear the story of their exemplary life?

What miracle was Mamie waiting for, she asked herself harshly. She had passed a healthy and reasonably happy life, for all she knew. She had a good family, and could even boast a great-grandchild, when she wasn't lamenting him. Her only ailment, if the Almighty really wanted to check, was jealousy.

Mamie had been a dutiful Catholic, but ritual doesn't demand much thought. The sudden moment of reflection was uncomfortable, but she was here and she would continue as piously as the next person. There was nothing else to do now.

They had queued at the entrance of the *Grotte* by now. Near by a young woman, heavily pregnant, was smiling and saying to a frail old gentleman, 'For the baby,' with a pat on her round belly.

Mamie thought of Marie. She liked the girl and decided that her thoughts would be for Marie and her baby, should anyone ask. She sat back in her chair, feeling pleased with herself for this unselfish thought. She would write it on her card to Julianna that she hadn't gone for herself. That would surely be one to beat.

Suddenly the young mother-to-be swayed, her eyes rolling up into her head.

'Catch her!' someone cried, but the girl had recovered.

'I'm all right, really I am,' she protested weakly. 'Please let me go in.'

Attendants had tried to lead her away to recover under supervision.

'Here,' came Mamie's gruff voice of authority, 'she can have my chair. I don't really need it.' It seemed so important to the girl and she certainly was in no condition to walk.

The crowd had begun to move forward and there was little time for argument. Mamie walked beside the girl, who reached up and silently squeezed her hand.

The family was assembled to meet Mamie's coach. As she greeted them she said simply, 'It's nice to be home.'

And to add substance to words, she once again began her old routines of feeding the poultry, tending her flowers and helping with the dinner.

Her roll of savings she put towards the addition Jacques had been working on for the growing family.

Mamie sent no picture postcards. She put those she'd bought into her box of mementoes, and never mentioned the trip again.

Who can say what they all thought of the change in Mamie? No doubt they said it was a miracle.

Finding Nina

The heat seemed to rise from the dusty clay road which bumped and bruised the soles of his feet, encased as they were in heavy leather city shoes. The countryside was bleached by the intense Gascon sun, denying any pleasure from the scenery, his crumpled linen suit was damp and stained from perspiration, and to top it all he was entirely covered with a fine layer of yellow pollen and dust. He sneezed.

And still the blasted path wound on before him, seeming not to know where it was going or to care when it got there. The woman in the *boulangerie* had said that he just couldn't miss it if he went this way. 'In this world or the next?' he wondered.

He was tired and thirsty. The confidence he had had as he stepped from the air conditioned coach in the heart of the village below was melting like the landscape before him in the shimmering sun.

What did he expect to find, a château or a hovel? And this Frenchwoman, would she speak English or would he have to rely on his schoolboy French? And how was he to begin? Still, he had come this far, into the furthest reaches of France, and he couldn't turn back now.

He squared his narrow shoulders and marched on. He was a slender young man, who would no doubt fill out his frame later in life. He was sandy-haired and fair, with hardly enough beard to warrant owning a razor even at twenty-one. He realized that he should have worn a hat, though he was too self-conscious to put his jacket over his head to shade his sun-baked head and face so he trudged on, utterly miserable.

At last a rosy roof came into view through the trees ahead. The lane was shaded for a while and he began to regain his composure. At the end of a stuccoed wall, he took off his jacket, smoothed his hair and prepared himself for whatever lay ahead. He boldly rounded the corner into the courtyard of the farmhouse, or what had once been a farmhouse.

The tastefully restored house and adjoining barn were obviously no longer part of a farm. Long windows opened from every room on to terraces where pots of cascading geraniums and canopies of grapevines altered the starkness of the house's treeless setting. In the distance, beyond the house, a group of women sat in a rose-covered summer-house. They had noticed him. Too late to run now.

At first glance the women appeared as daughter, mother and grand-mother, but at a closer view the older woman was not so old as just overweight, dressed in some sort of housemaid's pinafore which made him wonder whether she might be a servant. The youngest was probably no older than eighteen, although it was difficult to tell. She was sunning and left abruptly as he arrived. The older woman also retreated towards the house, carrying a tray with assorted glasses, her bleached curly hair bouncing along in time to her bottom.

There remained a slender, catlike woman lounging in a high-backed rattan chair. Her hair was almost black, streaked with the first white hairs which would describe her as 'distinguished'. Her eyes were up-turned slightly, giving them a touch of merriment, although she wasn't particularly smiling. With her hair cut short and blunt, she reminded him of a twenties' flapper. 'All she lacks,' he thought, 'is the cigarette holder.'

'Ah, you must be Richard,' she broke into a smile and extended her hand in greeting. She spoke English with a heavy French accent, calling him 'Ree-shard'.

'Do sit down. Flora will bring you a *citron pressé*. It is very good for the hots. Or if you wish, you can take off your clothes and bathe there,' she added pointing to a swimming pool behind a screen of bamboo where the girl was now bathing in the nude.

'No, no, I'm fine. A drink will do nicely,' he assured her quickly.

It surprised him to find that she seemed to have been expecting him. He immediately resented her casual familiarity. It wouldn't do her any good to pretend that she was some old friend of the family.

The pressed lemon juice arrived with a jug of iced water and a bowl of sugar. He mixed them to taste as he searched for a way to begin.

'Tell me how you are going now in school,' she began for him, lighting a cigarette held between long, thin fingers. He noticed her nails were painted blood red and that her light cotton dress fell sensually over the curves in her body. 'Hussy,' he thought.

'Um, you may or may not know,' Richard began awkwardly, 'my father passed away recently.'

'Yes, I know.' A shadow of intense emotion passed quickly over her face. 'I was very sad to hear of it.'

'I have reason to believe that ... to believe that you knew him ... well, intimately,' Richard went on.

'You say this very nicely, Richard.' She smiled at him with amusement. 'And what is it that makes you come so far to find me? To ask if it is true?'

'I'm afraid that a few things have been left unclear, and I thought perhaps we could discuss them,' Richard struggled to keep a businesslike tone to his voice. 'Father mentioned you, in a vague way, at the end,' he added resentfully.

His father had said, 'Find Nina,' without further explanation. Richard had taken no notice of this. His father surely didn't expect him to do anything for some unknown woman. That was, of course, until he had heard his father's will.

'Ah,' she savoured this. 'So I am a mystery and you have solved me! Now you must give me the denouement. Who am I then? It is most flattering to hear that I have inspired you to cross the Great English Channel, although I had rather expected that you might come eventually.'

She was laughing at him. He felt naïve and prudish and wished he had never come. But this business was important and he must go on, however painfully.

'I believe you were my father's mistress,' Richard said directly. 'Certain sums were paid regularly to the account of one N. Dubois whom I have traced to you here.'

'Not difficult.' She shook her head in mocking gravity.

'However,' he continued, raising his voice slightly, 'on his death, his business, our house, and even our car are now tied up in some trust, the principal trustee being that same N. Dubois!

'Forgive my indelicacy, but as his heir, I don't intend to stand by and see you inherit everything. And to add insult to injury, to accept a paltry allowance from your trust. I shall fight this, you can be sure!' Richard's hands were trembling and he stammered slightly.

'I see,' Nina murmured absently. She gazed into the distance towards the haze of mountains just barely visible.

'Is that all you have to say? My father was a rich man who sent me to the finest schools. I had been given every reason to believe that I would come into an inheritence which would ensure my future, and I still do!

'You've obviously had your share. It's plain to see that you did well out of him. I don't believe my father intended to ruin me in favour of you.' Richard was now quite close to tears.

'Dear Richard,' Nina began as smoothly as a spider. 'Poor Richard. How much you assume. Why do you suppose that you merit something that you have never worked for? Why does your mind logically conclude that if you were given a good education and material advantages that you would be given your living for the rest of your life? You are really very funny in your big talk, although I find you a little sad,' she pulled a discreet cord and Flora appeared.

'Flora, will you bring us a bottle of Colombel, *s'il te plaît*. There is some cold, I think. It is the hour for wine,' she added to Richard and then sank back in her chair, half shaded.

'Oh Richard, you are not as I thought you would be,' she continued sadly. His nerve was faltering and his lower lip trembled slightly.

'What does it matter anyway how you find me?' he replied defensively. 'What about you? How can a husband-stealing woman like you face her conscience? I just don't understand. My poor mother, left at home while he was always travelling. Travelling to be with you, I imagine. It's a blessing she didn't live to see this scandal.'

'What depresses me most about you, Richard, is your total lack of imagination,' Nina began languidly. 'But I suppose that was bred out of you in those "finest schools" of yours. All the jolly boys together, as they say. You are so stick-in-ze-mud!

'And your mother, she gave no love to him. She loved her ladies' coffees and her shopping. She wasn't a woman to miss a man, oh no.

'Have you no lovers? What would your father say about the way you are talking to me here? You talk the big man, but you know nothing about what you are talking. You make threats to get money and to hurt me. If your father loved me, why can you not be a little nice to me, Richard?'

She regarded him with a little pout. Flora arrived with the wine and the glasses.

'I apologize if I was rude,' Richard remarked without feeling. 'What did you expect me to think? It's all so terribly clear.'

'You pig-headed, over-educated, spoilt child, I feel sorry for you,' she said evenly. 'I expected you to come looking for the truth. Why else would your father have sent you to me? I feel sad that I didn't meet you myself earlier. Now maybe there's no hope.'

She had lost the affected air of simplicity and humour, and spoke coldly as he had done. He now regretted his error in his attack.

'OK,' Richard replied, being civil once more. 'Can you please explain how and why I've been disinherited? That is really the question I'm asking. It's nothing really to do with you personally.'

He sat back in his chair and gazed into the distance, avoiding her eyes. 'Cat eyes,' he thought, 'and I'm her afternoon mouse.'

'Oh but I'm afraid that it has everything to do with me, as you say, personally,' she mused, pouring out wine for them both. He thought for a moment that she intended to say no more.

'Where shall I ever begin? Your father has not helped me much, I see. All our dark past comes back to haunt us, does it not?

'My father was a wealthy businessman and I was his only child. My mother died when I was a little girl and my aunt came to live with us to look after me. I did not take well to school or governesses,' she added.

Richard sniffed at this personal addition and she continued with more reserve.

'And so when I was twenty and my father hired a handsome young accountant, I fell in love. We fell in love. My father was furious. He waited for a great match for me, so he sent me away with my aunt on a grand tour.

'It is so tedious, the travelling. Always another museum, another garden or statue that is good for you to look at. Like a very long art history class.

'When I came home he had arranged a marriage for the young accountant and given him a promotion. He had had little choice. My father said that the young Englishman didn't know how lucky he was because he was poor and the girl was from a family with high social connections.

'So when I was painting in my studio, my aunt could arrange for my lover to meet me. When he travelled, I could make some excuse to go away and be with him. It was such a naughty, happy time.'

She paused and smiled reflectively while Richard continued to look away.

'My poor mother,' he commented. 'I doubt whether it was a happy time for her.'

'When my father died,' she continued briskly, 'the business came to me. I put my lover, your father, in charge and took a discreet allowance for my living. After all, it is a man's business. I gave him everything he wanted — a big house, the sports cars that he loved — I could never refuse him anything.' She laughed and shook her head. 'But these things must come back to me now, as you can see. And that is what was arranged.

'Did your father ever talk to you about the business?' she asked curiously.

'Something about properties and hotels, isn't it?' Richard replied offhandedly. 'I thought someone else managed it, actually.'

'Yes,' she admitted slowly. 'Hotels, yes. My dear naïve Richard, I don't know how to explain these delicate things to you.'

She sat covering a distinct giggle with her hand.

'Your father managed my brothels, hotels with lovely ladies, where parties would go on all night with great and important men from all over the world. They were beautiful hotels, with red velvet everywhere and crystal chandeliers that always sparkled. Your father took me to see them when my father would never have allowed me inside. It was such fun, and so gay.

'So much has changed in the last ten or fifteen years. Once there were five and now there are only two. And they must do a restaurant as well as a bar to keep up appearances. Your father started an escort service, which is doing very well, but it isn't the same. In the old days the ladies had a real home and a family. And they knew that they would be looked after if they had children or when they were sick or old.

'That is why we have the trust. It looks after everyone, like Flora, like you. Great men have shares in the trust, and when they die, their shares come back as a bequest. It is very discreet, you see,' she remarked with a raised eyebrow.

Richard was visibly shaken. She quickly refilled his glass and looked on anxiously as he drank thoughtfully shaking his head from time to time in disbelief.

'So that's it,' he said finally with an air of resignation. 'There was no family business for me to inherit.'

'Tell me what you would have done if there was, Richard?' Nina asked curiously. 'You could not have thought to run it yourself, and you have shown no interest in it.'

'Well, I have friends from school, you see,' he began, 'and we had an idea we'd do some business together. One chap's father is in investments and we have the inside tips. We could make a bomb on the stock market.

'Then there's this girl. Her father's worth a title and a bit, but I'd have to look like money to catch her. And I could have if I'd had the family business.' Richard was now feeling sorry for himself.

Nina looked towards heaven.

'But Richard, what of an occupation? What did you think you would really do with all the long days? And you talk about a girl, but no love. You are ruined before you begin!' She threw up her hands in a hopeless gesture.

'Did your parents tell you that you were adopted?' she asked suddenly.

'Of course they did. I was a foundling. Oh God! What are you saying?' He half rose in horror at the ideas which flew through his head.

'When I was ... when we were expecting a baby, we were so happy, even though I knew my father could never know and that I couldn't keep the child with me. We stayed here together for a while with my aunt, then I went away and, *voilà*, we found a lovely baby. He was so happy when it was a boy. Your mother was too frail to have children, so they adopted you. I hope she never knew. But as I said, I never could deny him anything,' she laughed.

Richard's mouth hung open and he sat with both hands on the chair as if he meant to rise.

They looked at one another for some time.

'Richard, I'm your mother,' she said softly, kindly, without touching him.

'I'm in a bad film!' He laughed incredulously.

'Perhaps for you,' she said curtly, 'but also for me. There is so much to be done with you and I have been too much absent in the influence. I can hear your father in your wild schemes.

'But now you must have something to eat. A boy needs a good meal after such a day. And of course you will want to meet your sister. When my father died we had our second child...'

Richard stood still. The rich golden light of the afternoon swirled colours before his eyes. He looked down into the dark, loving eyes of Nina and fainted.

The Movie

'Come along, Tattie,' a tired woman of middle age urged her frail old aunt in a hearty voice. 'We'll be late.'

The deaf woman stared vacantly into her coffee bowl. Hers was always the one with the crack, she was thinking.

Her niece looked from time to time out the window as people began gathering in the street below.

'We'll be late,' she repeated and firmly but gently pulled her aunt from her chair.

Etrangers, foreigners, were making a movie in their village today. It was based on stories of the war, they said, and they wanted old Tattie to be in it. The niece shook her head with exasperation as the old woman shuffled slowly towards the door, muttering to herself. These people must be mad, she thought, to ask an old, senile woman to be in a movie. Still, it was well paid.

When the two women finally reached the church square, the film crew were already busy at work. A group of men worked at laying huge electrical cables, just as they did for the fairs, while villagers in costumes of the old times lounged about on shiny vintage cars brought into the village on huge, flat-bedded *camions*. Tattie didn't need a costume. She dressed as she always had done in black with a black shawl. A local farmer in smock and sabots tended his yoke of oxen. Several older people stood in little groups, obviously waiting for orders. Everyone would be paid, they said, and not to forget the thrill of seeing yourself in the movies.

The bell tolled the hour. An actor dressed in a cassock as a *curé* leant against the Gothic arch of the church porch, smoking a cigarette. Tattie obediently pulled her black shawl over her head as if to enter.

'Sit her there, on those steps under the cross, as if she's just waiting for someone,' the Director shouted. A second man translated these orders.

'Now you just wait for me a few minutes, Tattie,' the niece instructed as she helped her aunt to sit on the cold stone. As she walked away she looked back to be sure the old woman had understood, but she seemed sunk in her dream state and unlikely to wander off.

The dried old woman was, in fact, watching the sunlight play on the geraniums in the window boxes of the houses around the square. Their vivid reds and corals were so clear to her today. And how pink the bricks were. It must be summer.

Suddenly a burst of light blanched the scene. Everything became stark and colourless and ugly. The old woman squinted nervously and rose to hurry away, but a man in uniform took her by the arm and sat her back in her place to wait. She could not understand his words, but she nodded. She must wait.

'They've come again,' she said to herself recognizing the uniform, 'but I won't tell.'

A bus rumbled slowly past. There was something about it that she remembered. What a lovely little hat the lady inside was wearing. She remembered travelling to Agen on a bus like that one.

Then from a side street soldiers in a troop carrier appeared, driving at full speed. With guns raised and much shouting they stopped the bus crying, 'Papers!'

'Cut!' cried the Director. The entire scene went slowly into reverse as the soldiers backed away out of sight and the bus creaked backwards past the old woman.

Forward came the bus and its passengers once more, and again the soldiers waited for them. 'Papers!' Again and again the scene repeated itself beneath the strong Gascon sun and the foreign lights.

Tattie sat and waited. She wondered if her niece would come on the next bus. She looked to see if she knew anyone else, but each time the passengers were the same.

Suddenly a shot rang out. Soldiers flooded the square, running with guns. People were pulled from the bus and thrown against it, hands over their heads. A man was singled out.

Memories flooded back so clearly now, like the tears she had shed so long ago. It was all happening again, just as she had always tried to blot it from her nightmares.

They had stopped their bus from Agen as if for a routine check of papers, then it had happened. Soldiers had pulled them from the bus at gunpoint.

The Resistance had struck in the night and had killed several enemy soldiers. Where were they? Who were they?

A first man was shot as an example.

She had stood with her husband, too horrified to make a cry. He had stood calmly, holding her hand to steady her. She must not tell.

Where were the Resistance hiding? It would go easier if someone were to speak. There would be reprisals. They would shoot double the number of villagers as soldiers who were killed. Speak!

They pulled her husband from her side. Where are they hiding?

'You must not tell,' his eyes told her.

Then they had shot him.

She stood on frail legs on the step below the cross, in the midst of the movie set, fists clenched by her cheeks and screamed.

'Zoom in on the old lady!' the Director cried excitedly. Cameras turned and everyone watched as the old woman's face twisted with some terrible memory. She was speaking, walking forward with her hands outstretched in some pleading gesture towards the soldiers.

Then she collapsed.

'Cut! What a chance that was.' The Director whistled as local people scurried for help. The false *curé* was first to her side, propping Tattie's head up as people searched for her niece.

Tattie was murmuring almost incomprehensibly now.'I didn't tell. They shot my husband but I never would tell. They were with us, you see. The Resistance were hiding in our barn. I didn't tell.

'I know I am dying, Father, because you have been dead all these years. They shot you later for betraying us that day. So it must have been a sin to be silent, if you are with me now. But if I am bound for hell, with my last breath, I spit on you!'

As she did so, she smiled up into the face of the false *curé* with satisfaction and died.

'What was that all about?' somebody asked as the ambulance was driving away.

'How should I know? I don't think she was even speaking French,' the actor replied gruffly, hurrying to rid himself of the cassock.

Outside the café on the square the actors and film crew sat over beer. The café owner had never had so much business and was rushing to and fro as he struggled to get the orders right. The villagers lined up to receive their pay as extras from a brisk young woman with a stack of banknotes in front of her amidst the crew's beer glasses.

The bell in the tower began to toll, not for the hour, but for the end of hours. It tolled for the dead, telling the valleys that every soul has a story and an ending. For a moment the bell stopped the action in the square as the devout crossed themselves and others turned their heads toward the church instinctively following the compulsive, doleful sound.

The niece came forward and held out her hand. 'For my aunt,' she demanded simply.

The purser checked the list for the amount due and the girl counted it out. Awkwardly she added her condolences.

The villagers disappeared, some to their chores, others to their meal. The film crew relaxed at the café.

'When does this thing come out?' someone asked.

'Not until next year, I think,' replied the purser.

'Hope they don't all go spare like that old woman when they see it,' said the actor who had been with Tattie at the end. He was still shaken.

'Oh most of them will probably get a kick out of it all,' the first laughed. 'After all, it will make the whole thing look a lot more exciting than it really was.'

The shadows grow quickly in the narrow medieval streets of the village, where wash water still pours from the front of the brick and timber houses into a central channel in the cobbles and 'night soil' is still carried in tin buckets in the early hours. Shutters are drawn against the light and against the dark, and there are secrets behind them that will never be told.

The Perfect Match

Thiabald d'Asterac was not an ordinary young man. Unlike the others of his age in the village, he stood apart, by his education at a private school, by his birth into an old and aristocratic family and by virtue of his being his widowed mother's only son.

If Thiabald's encounters with his local contemporaries were rare, it must be said that his encounters with local girls were rarer. In fact, encounters with any but the most refined and eligible young ladies simply did not occur.

At twenty-four, Thiabald was dark, reasonably good-looking and extremely aware of his social advantage. On this particular spring morning as he strolled through the village market purely out of boredom, his perfume floated after him, turning the heads of women, young and old. He was well-dressed in expensive casual clothes as a wealthy young law student, home for a holiday, might be. Occasionally someone stopped him to bid him good-day and to ask politely after his studies and his dear mother. He tried to avoid such meetings.

He had been told that he lacked the common touch. In truth it was that he loathed to touch the common.

The sound of a flute caught the young man's attention as he entered the square by the church. A silhouetted figure stood just in the far shadows, bending gracefully as a willow twig to an aria from *Orpheus*.

Thiabald propped himself against a pillar of the covered arcade to enjoy the scene. The music changed everything. It was no longer an ordinary market, but a scene of some theatrical performance, the people noble representatives of the simple life. He mused over these new impressions, savouring the smells and colours for the first time he could remember since his childhood.

The flautist ended the impromptu concert. Thiabald approached to make a contribution to the open flute case and to exchange a few words with someone whom he felt sure must be as cultured as himself.

'Very nice,' remarked Thiabald, casually dropping a ten franc piece into the velvet-lined case. To his surprise, the flautist was a young woman who regarded him with large, haughty dark eyes.

'Thank-you,' she replied simply in a soft voice, with no trace of a local accent.

'It must be difficult playing in a place like this,' he commented with a slight nod and a sneer towards some of the passing peasant farmers.

'Any why?' she asked curtly, stopping in her collection of pages of music. 'These people are more receptive than some stuffy concert hall audiences I've known.'

'Then you play in concert,' he said with interest. 'Where?'

'I play where I'm invited. Sometimes Paris, sometimes other places, sometimes in the streets. I like to practise with an audience. Now, excuse me, I must go.'

'Will you have a drink with me first?' Thiabald asked directly, surprised at his boldness with this curious stranger.

'Yes, I suppose,' she replied, eyeing him cautiously.

That afternoon over tea with his mother on the flower-decked terrace Thiabald could speak only of the flautist.

'And she's played with the orchestra in Paris,' he nodded with emphasis. 'She lives there now, although it isn't originally her home. She grew up in Switzerland, near Lake Geneva.'

'Thiabald,' his mother stopped him with an exasperated smile, 'I haven't heard you half so excited about anything since the first time you rode a train!'

'But, *Mère*, you're always saying that I should interest myself more in people,' he protested, 'and now I'm absolutely fascinated!'

'And what is your young virtuoso called, then?' his mother smiled indulgently.

'I didn't actually ask,' he confessed. 'It was all rather awkward.'

'Well, are you planning to see this young lady again?'

'I didn't arrange anything, actually.' Thiabald frowned slightly at his own inexperience with such matters. 'I'll have to see if she plays again at the market.'

'She plays at the market?' his mother looked shocked. 'You don't mean to say that she's one of those street beggars?'

'Oh no!' he replied with feeling. 'She just enjoys practising in front of an audience and thinks that the peasants respond well to music. You can't imagine what a different it seems to make in their shopping.'

'I hardly think … ' his mother began with a deep breath, 'that the young lady is what one might call "suitable".'

Mme d'Asterac was a straight woman. That is to say that everything about her seemed to align itself vertically from the aristocratic aquiline bridge of her nose to the fall of her favourite ebony beads. Her feminine anatomy made no impression on the line of her monochrome clothes, and even the sweep of her now-greying hair which she wore securely fastened in a knot at the nape of her neck continued the effect to such an extent that she gave the impression of being taller than she actually was.

She was from the North, meaning north of the Loire which divides France in so many ways. She had been raised to know and live with what it was to be an aristocrat in a country without an aristocracy. Life for her had existed in a cocoon of her own kind, behind iron gates which protected them all from the taint of ordinary life. Her marriage into an ancient Gascon family was the best match that could be arranged at the time, and had been successful as well as happy.

Thiabald was her joy. An intelligent young man with great prospects, he represented the last of both sides of his noble ancestors. When his education was finished, his mother would begin in earnest to find a perfect match for him.

Thiabald returned to Paris to his studies and the flautist had all but been forgotten when a letter from him mentioned in a postscript, 'Met Isolde again — you remember the flautist? We had quite an evening at all the best places. You'll adore her. We'll be down next weekend.'

His mother felt defensive and cross for no reason. Jealousy, she told herself, but realized that it was genuine concern at her son's first true romance.

'And we don't know a thing about her,' she confided to her dearest friend. 'I would feel so much better if he had had a few infatuations before this one. He seems so — decided.'

'Time will tell,' her friend replied sagely if slightly absently. After all, she had had her share of disastrous romances amongst her own children.

But Isolde was a perfect lady, charming, fresh and natural. Her conversation was entertaining and varied, and she seemed as devoted to Thiabald as he was to her. The weekend was a great success.

'And, my dear,' Mme d'Asterac told her friend at their next meeting, 'she was completely educated at home. Her knowledge of the philosophers is quite extraordinary. That does speak of a certain class of family, does it not? As for her flute — private lessons with some of the best performing artists alive today. They all want to know her. Her mother was great friends with ... oh what is that conductor's name?'

Thiabald's mother was enjoying her little boast about this most exceptional creature her son had discovered.

'She loves to travel. Hates steamers. Found the train to Bavaria a pleasure — and I can appreciate that — and we have Italy in common!'

'My dear,' said her friend leaning forward in her chair to give advice, 'aren't you being just a bit, shall I say, unguarded? A few concrete facts about the child wouldn't hurt, now would they? And then you can happily let the romance develop.'

'You are always a wise counsel,' Mme d'Asterac sighed in agreement. 'I shall make some enquiries.'

But to Mme d'Asterac's great delight, Isolde's family name in Lake Geneva was even more aristocratic than their own. She now sat anxiously hoping that her son wouldn't let such a catch slip away.

Far away in Paris, however, as the couple sat close to one another at a candlelit table in a little bistro, Isolde was saying, 'No, Thiabald, I cannot marry you. We are from such different backgrounds, I could only be an embarrassment to you.'

'Nonsense,' Thiabald replied, 'our backgrounds aren't dependent on money or important parents. Our education, travel, common interests — that is the background that counts.'

'Exactly, *mon amour*,' she said with sadness in her large dark eyes, 'you have seen so little of the world, and I have seen so much.'

And so they parted. Thiabald was shattered, his mother indignant.

'So the young lady feels that she is too good for my son,' Mme d'Asterac fumed to her friend as she recounted the latest gossip. 'Time did tell. Things are not always as they seem.'

'Haste makes waste,' her friend put in vacantly. 'I'm truly sorry, but you know, I think sometimes we forget how provincial we are in our little village. Why should it surprise us if an educated, talented young lady with every prospect before her has no interest in burying herself in a forgotten village lost in the hills of old Gascony?' She chuckled a little and added, 'I wasn't all that pleased to come here myself, if you must know, but in my day a rich husband was a rich husband.'

They nodded solemnly over this fact of life.

'Perhaps you could find the girl and have a chat,' the friend suggested in a flash of inspiration.

'But what would I say?'

'Oh, perhaps suggest a long engagement, that they take some time and travel to get to know one another. You could hint at a law practice for Thiabald in Toulouse. Do you really want to keep this girl or not? Use some imagination!'

'You're right, of course,' Mme d'Asterac replied in something of a dither. 'She's such a catch, and she'd advance Thiabald's career no end. He can be so stuffy on his own. But just imagine how silly I'll feel chasing after her in Paris! I don't have a thing to wear, I'm sure.'

But the strategy was finally planned. Madame would go to Paris under the pretext of visiting her son. It would be quite natural then to call on Isolde. If her clothes were slightly out of date, then so much the better. This could be a fine old Gascon custom for all anyone knew.

The train was smooth and the trip uneventful. She arrived at the *Gare* Austerlitz to find it much the same as she remembered it from years ago. With a shiver of excitement she sat down at the station café for a cup of coffee.

She raised a gloved hand discreetly as a grey-haired waiter waltzed smoothly past. He stopped two tables away, apparently not noticing her.

'*Garçon*,' she called politely the next time he passed. He stopped with a scowl.

'If Madame will observe, I am attending each table in turn. After the next table it will be the turn of Madame.' His patronizing tone and superior bearing gave the impression that he might be someone of her own class, fallen on hard times. He turned with his nose in the air. A table of young people laughed. She noticed that no one wore gloves. Dropping her hands into her lap, she removed the gloves and waited patiently for the waiter, feeling slightly less confident.

Thiabald met his mother there as arranged.

'My darling, you're looking pale,' cooed Mme d'Asterac as she greeted him with kisses on both cheeks.

'I've had quite a bit of work to do recently.' He dismissed her fuss.

'Then I don't suppose you've seen Isolde lately. How is she?' his mother enquired offhandedly.

'No, I don't have much time to see her just now,' he replied, looking forlornly away.

'Worse than expected,' she thought.

'Perhaps then while you're busy I might just pop round for a coffee and say hallo. I planned to do some shopping while I'm here so it would be nice to stop to see her.'

'I'll give you her number,' Thiabald said without interest. 'She's often away on concert trips, or just seeing the country, as she puts it. She lives with a Mme Dupont. I believe she is usually at home.'

Mme d'Asterac decided to make a visit in person. It was difficult to refuse to speak to someone face to face. Besides, she was curious to see where and with whom Isolde lived.

The address led to a faded old building in what had once been a fashionable part of the town. A door led into a courtyard, now overgrown where a fine old entrance opened into an even finer old lobby. A sweeping stairway wound up through the building and led eventually to the number Thiabald had given her. She pressed the bell.

It was some time before the door opened and a dark, haughty woman with short cropped hair appeared. She held a cigarette and was clad in black leggings and an enormous orange sweater which came nearly to her knees. The mother was reminded of pictures she'd seen of beatniks.

'Good-morning,' Mme d'Asterac said pleasantly, 'I'm looking for Isolde. Are you Mme Dupont?'

The woman eyed her for a moment and took a long drag from her cigarette before answering.

'You must be Thiabald's mother. Won't you come in?' she invited in a husky voice without a trace of a smile.

Mme d'Asterac had the impression of entering a tent. The flat was hung with oriental tapestries. Cushions covered the corners of the floor, and low tables and statues forced her to watch her step.

Mme Dupont gestured towards a cushion-covered divan and Mme d'Asterac sat.

'Let me get you something to drink. Vodka? Whisky? Wine?' she offered, still without a smile.

'She's had a face-lift,' thought Mme d'Asterac, observing the lack of expression around her eyes and mouth. 'How extraordinary she looks — as if she were wearing a mask.'

'Just a little wine, please,' Mme d'Asterac requested, slightly surprised because of the early hour.

'And now.' Mme Dupont curled up in her corner with a large vodka and regarded the other woman as if she were the most fascinating person she had seen for ages. It was most disconcerting.

'I was just in town to see my son, so I thought I'd call on Isolde as I passed.'

'Yes, I see,' the other regarded her with the same unhelpful, fixed stare.

'She's a lovely child, Isolde, and I've so enjoyed her visits to me. Are you a relation? She said that she is an orphan.' Mme d'Asterac tried to make conversation.

'So are we all in this world!' Mme Dupont declared with a burst of conviction. 'The act of love and of birth are but accidents of nature and so we are alone from the moment the cord is cut.

'What do most parents do for their children? They live their own lives again through them as if they were puppets! They feed them rusty rules and selected experiences. And what then becomes of these children? They become the adults who repeat the dreadful cycle!'

Mme Dupont sat with her eyes very wide and round, but with no other expression. Mme d'Asterac wondered if this outburst required a response, but decided that conventional manners were hardly required. She wished she had asked for something stronger as she sipped her wine and affected a look of concerned agreement, hoping to avoid any further outburst.

'But you have not said why you have really come,' Mme Dupont continued. 'Is it because Isolde has refused your son? I only guess, but I know she has stopped seeing him.'

'Well, yes,' Mme d'Asterac confessed. 'I simply wanted to ask her to reconsider his proposal of marriage. I like her very much, and it would be a pity if she had refused because of some misunderstanding.'

Mme Dupont regarded her for some time as if deciding whether or not to comment on this. Finally she gave a long, patient sigh and put her glass on the floor. Sitting up, cross-legged as a Buddha, she said, 'You are conventional people. Isolde is not. You would have her say "yes" to your boy, but that is "yes" only to remain the same for ever. One step from your definition of a lovely girl and you will not be so fond of her.'

Mme Dupont lit another cigarette and looked deeply into the eyes of Mme d'Asterac.

'I should be going now,' Mme d'Asterac said rather sharply. 'Thank-you for the wine.'

'I will tell Isolde that you came,' said Mme Dupont rising gracefully from the floor. 'She will be pleased.'

'It's for the best,' Mme d'Asterac assured her son. 'To have grown up like ... like a gypsy ... well, I just don't know. And as for that woman, I deeply suspect her to be the child's natural mother! Heaven forbid!'

Although Mme d'Asterac's trip may have been in her terms a good end to bad business, it prompted Isolde to telephone Thiabald. In their favourite corner café they sat and talked.

'I didn't want to hurt you with tedious explanations,' Isolde said earnestly. 'I thought you would just go away and find another girl like nice, normal boys do.'

'But you see? I'm not so normal as you thought,' he smiled. 'Does that mean I have potential?'

'Potential for what?'

'For becoming whatever sort of man of the world you would prefer,' he said with a shrug.

'It's only that I've lived such an adventurous life. My mother was a dancer and didn't believe in marriage or in mothering, really. I've had wonderful advantages, but it does make me shy of conventions,' she confessed.

'My education has been through experiences. If someone recommended a book, I read it; if someone was willing to show me how to do something, I tried it. If I liked something, I worked to master it.

'Playing my flute in the street for poor people, dressing up grandly for the opera, taking an ocean liner when I could have taken a plane, all are marvellous experiences. Even meeting you and your mother with all your provincial snobbery is an experience. But my life can't stop there, you know.' She put her hand over his.

'Then let me suggest some other experiences for you,' Thiabald said. 'How about travelling about, having experiences as two instead of as one, of teaching a stuffy old law student something expressive for his spare time? What about choosing and decorating your own house or having a baby and watching it grow?

'It would be sad if you let your mother repeat her life in you. It seems to me that we grow up reflecting our parents lives just so far and then we go on to do our own version. What do you think?'

'I think you'll make an excellent lawyer,' she laughed with tears in her eyes as she leant over the table and kissed him.

And so Isolde accepted Thiabald. At the news Mme Dupont retired with a bottle of vodka and Mme d'Asterac fled to her friend's for tea, or even something stronger.

The Secret

The bell in the nearby church tower dully sounded twice. She lay still in the elaborately carved bed feeling like a child, small and frightened. It was cold and she was alone.

From somewhere below she imagined she could hear someone's steps, but she knew it was her imagination. The house was far too vast to hear what might be happening below. Yet she knew that he was down there, as he was so often at night. His work, he would say, and yet what could a *notaire* be doing at this hour of the morning? She had learnt not to ask questions of her husband, even in the short time they had been married. He was a much older man, and she knew the extent of his anger when she annoyed me.

She wondered when he would come back to bed and was relieved to hear his footsteps coming along the corridor at last.

He entered the room quietly and closed the door. He had two suitcases with him which he left in the middle of the room.

'Get up,' he said in a flat whisper without making any pretext of waking her. 'I know you are awake. Get the baby. We're going away.'

She stared at him in disbelief.

'Albert, what has happened?' she whispered.

'They are accusing those of us who have had dealings with the Germans of being collaborators. I have had word that they may come for me as soon as tomorrow.'

'But that's ridiculous,' she said with uncertainty. 'What else could you have done? You would have been shot by the Germans if you hadn't co-operated.'

'You don't know half of what has happened in that office, Yvette.' He gazed about the room at the fine draperies with their gold trim, the costly antiques, and shook his head. 'There are secrets which passed there that men have paid dearly to have kept, and secrets men have paid handsomely to possess.'

'But I've done nothing,' she began as panic seized her. 'Leave us behind. You can go faster alone. I don't want to live like a gypsy, to be on the run like a criminal or to hide in some foreign country. They don't have anything against me.'

'You must come, you are my cover,' he replied coldly. 'Besides, you are wrong if you think you could stay here, Madame. After they ransack the house for the jewellery and treasures I've appropriated and find nothing, they will surely have their revenge. Or perhaps I should leave you two to take the peasants' wrath. Fancy losing your head like a true aristocrat, my beauty?'

He towered over her, a grey-haired man fifteen years her senior. She was young and sheltered and had made 'a good match'. She had had comforts even throughout the war, never knowing or considering where they might have come from. Now she cowered at the thought of what this could mean.

'Come with me,' he ordered roughly.

Lighting an oil lamp and holding it in one hand, he grasped her arm firmly and hurried her along the back passage of the house. Quiet as a thief so as not to awaken the maid, he lifted the latch to the cellar door and they descended.

The damp, cold air smelled rancid with saltpetre. She shivered and drew her lacy bed shawl tighter around her shoulders. From the shadows, creatures darted in and out of the feeble light, but she dared not scream.

Albert stopped before a row of ancient casks which had once held the household wine. He bent and reached under one of these, releasing a metal catch holding a section of the barrel supports. Slowly he now moved one of the dark, dirty barrels out on its supports, revealing a brick wall covered in grime. Yvette shivered once more but strained forward to see what her husband might do next.

Any trace of a door was obscured by the shadows thrown in the deep recesses worn between the bricks. With practised skill, Albert inserted a long, thin key between two bricks and finding the hole, turned it easily. With only a muffled noise, soft as the intake of breath, a doorway opened before him.

Ducking his head and holding the lamp before him, the *Notaire* stooped to enter a tiny room. It must have at one time been part of another, smaller vault, perhaps one older than the house itself, his wife thought. Now it resembled a pirate's treasure store. Paintings and ornaments of value cluttered the recess, but Albert had already selected a small chest, ignoring the rest.

'There, my spoiled and pampered one,' he laughed coldly, holding the lamp high to show the contents to advantage. 'This is my treasure. There are gold and jewels to keep me for a few years, I'll wager. And deeds, the inheritances of dead men now. You see how it can be to have "friends" during a war.'

He looked mad in the lamplight. His sharp laugh sounded forced as the import of it all began to sink in.

'Then it wasn't your family's money,' she said slowly. 'You have betrayed your neighbours, let them be shot, and then taken their money. You really are a criminal of the war.' She waited dully for confirmation.

'Family fortune?' he asked in disbelief, ignoring her accusations. 'I was penniless until I met your father. He had a rather guilty conscience, you see. He was most generous, even to the extent of throwing his little girl into the bargain in the hope of appeasing me.'

Now he laughed heartlessly and she saw the truth for the first time: their meeting in her father's study during 'some business', her father's sudden preoccupation with her marriage, his generosity towards them and his tragic worrying which finally was his end.

'You're vile!' she spat at him, but he was preoccupied with transferring as much as possible from the chest into a waiting suitcase.

As she regarded him fixedly, she began to withdraw from the vault. Perhaps it had once been a crypt, she thought vaguely as she pulled the well-oiled door easily closed behind her and turned the key. She heard him call to her, but now was not the time to be faint-hearted. What did she want? Revenge for her father and his betrayal? Would she tell them of his whereabouts?

In tears of confusion she replaced the barrel and then stumbling blindly through the darkness, found the stairway and escape.

The maid waited outside the bedroom door the next morning while the doctor attended the *Notaire*'s wife. Feverish, she refused any food. Monsieur the Doctor was certain that she was suffering from some shock. Each time the *Notaire* was mentioned, Madame became quite agitated. She seemed frightened, they thought. Had her husband threatened her before he disappeared, or was it that she was fearing the wrath of the village upon herself and the child?

'We must treat her gently for a while, I think,' reported the Doctor to the housemaid and the head of the local police charged with arresting the *Notaire*.

'But you must let us question her!' the burly man cried angrily. 'We must find the man and punish him. After all, she's his wife, isn't she? And nobody noticed her disapproval of his ill-got fortune or of his German friends, for that matter.'

Tempers were high and had it not been for the Doctor's reasoning that kindness might gain more information than violence, the people waiting outside the house might have attacked her there and then.

But the *Notaire*'s wife lay in a delirious state for several days, her sweet-tempered baby charming those who had taken him in care.

In the end, the inevitable questioning was not so bad as she had feared. It was generally now believed that the *Notaire* had fled with the aid of an accomplice, perhaps even another woman, leaving his wife and child to take the blame in his place. She had the sympathy of many as she appeared so young without her elegant clothes and coiffed hair. A young mother with a baby had nothing to fear from the tribunal, they assured her.

A new *notaire* was appointed. Yvette was allowed to remain in a part of the house, while the offices were given over to the new *Notaire*.

Yvette lived simply and frugally, learning the work in the office to help support herself and the young Louis. It was generally agreed that she had suffered in her first marriage.

Claud, the new *Notaire*, was a well-liked son of the village, of humble origins and a hard-won education. People grasped his hand eagerly in the streets. He was not so tall nor so distinguished as Albert, but he had a captivating smile and a generous nature which were to his credit.

When time had passed, Claud purchased the house and married the abandoned wife of the now almost forgotten Albert, adopting little Louis, to the approving nods of the villagers.

Claud became a devoted husband and father, grew round and

agreeable with age, and after an uneventful career, handed his office to his son on his retirement.

Yvette remained thrifty and level-headed, understanding the value of keeping the common touch, thrilling to the pleasure of charity and a sterling reputation. She was a strong, confident woman, fortified by the secret knowledge that she had avenged the village and that everyone's secrets would remain buried in the crypt in the cellar for ever, guarded by a dead man.

In time, the house and family property were put into the name of Louis, as is the custom to avoid death duties. He was obliged only to look after his parents under his roof until they died. The secret need never be told, Yvette decided, unless they had need.

Life, unfortunately, is never so simple.

It was during the cheese course of one ordinary midday meal that Louis announced, 'I have been thinking of selling the house.'

Yvette and Claud sat and stared in disbelief. Their lives had remained happily stagnant and dependable for all this time because they had worked to keep it so. Now their son had breathed the forbidden word, 'change'.

'I know what you must be thinking,' he put up his hands to stop comment, 'but it's a wise move. The town is changing, and my office is too far from the new commercial centre of town.

'The house needs quite a bit of work — its foundations were never strong — and that will cost quite a bit.'

He now lost a bit of his confident tone and added rather shyly, 'Also, I thought that should I ever marry,' he coughed with embarrassment, 'it would be nice to have a house divided into separate apartments. I've actually seen just the place.'

His parents still sat like statues, not betraying any emotion. He continued, speaking slightly faster. 'I took the liberty of contacting an agent, you see. Or rather, he contacted me. It seems that there is someone who wants to buy this house, if we will sell it. The letter said that the client was here during the war and remembered it. It's a good offer, and so I started thinking about it seriously.'

'Marry?' Yvette asked with a growing smile. She hadn't heard a word since the mention of that much-hoped-for possibility. Her mind was tumbling with thoughts of grandchildren and all their future happiness.

Claud took his cue from his wife and lumbered off to find something to celebrate with.

'Is it Natalie?' Yvette demanded with excitement. She liked the girl and Louis often saw her.

'Stop, Mother,' Louis said sternly. 'I said **if** I were to marry.'

Claud returned and they popped a cork on a bottle of sparkling wine. They drank to their good fortune, to the new house and to Yvette's dream of grandchildren.

'When will the buyer come to look over the house?' enquired Claud.

'He's sending an agent to take care of things for him, if we agree,' Louis explained.

'Well then, what's the man's name, at least, and where does he come from?' Claud asked good-humouredly.

'Just a minute,' Louis took out a piece of paper. 'I have a letter. He's an American. It says he's buying it for his daughter and son-in-law and hopes to spend some time here himself one day. The name is A. Jones.'

'American enough,' replied Claud thoughtfully.

It was after the preliminaries to the sale that Yvette noticed something that left her with an odd chill.

'They are his initials, just as he used to sign them!' She fretted nervously. 'I'd know them anywhere. But it couldn't be...'

She thought of the vault in the cellar and wondered what she should do. Try to destroy some of the documents? Recover some of the fortune for Louis? Or leave it all with its ghostly guardian for the new owners to find whenever they reinforced the foundations.

Claud sat slumped beside the fire. Yvette regretted mentioning Albert, for after all, there was no danger of him coming back. But it seemed that this must be the time for her confession, to reassure her husband.

'Claud,' she began in a halting voice, 'Albert can never come back. I locked him in the hidden vault downstairs and left him. You are married to a very wicked woman.'

Yvette began to weep softly, not out of regret and remorse but out of having to tell Claud, who had always thought her good.

'Yvette, Yvette!' He gently took her in his arms. 'Don't cry. You're not the murderess you think you are. There, there now.'

'Oh, Claud,' she put her arms around his neck. 'It was just so horrible — and I ...'

'It would have been better if you had, my dear,' he sighed, 'but I, too, have a little confession.

'You see, my family were cheated out of their land by Monsieur the

Notaire. It was my father who knew of the vault behind the wall because he had worked to seal it off for the previous owners. And he knew well enough how their estate passed into the hands of the *Notaire*!

'So when we heard that they were going to arrest him — and would have probably shot him after all the honest people he'd betrayed — I decided to try to find my grandfather's deeds.

'I knew he'd have to hide his illegal files in the vault. They would surely sack his office. So I came in through your kitchen early in the morning. The key was in the vault as if I'd been expected. I couldn't believe it when I opened the door and found him there! I nearly shot him in fright.

'Yes, I'm no fool. I had a gun, so we came to a little agreement. For a considerable sum, including my own family's inheritance, I would help him escape and arrange for money to be put into a bank account for him in America.'

Claud's voice trailed off and he smiled slightly, like a wicked boy.

Yvette sat open-mouthed in amazement.

'All this time I thought I was keeping a terrible secret, that I had avenged the wrong Albert had done. And all this time Albert and his fortune were in America!' she laughed bitterly.

'But I'm afraid Albert's fortune didn't exactly join him in America. Oh, it was years before I finally sold and invested it all. He must have been terribly cross to find that for the first time in his life, someone double-crossed *him*. I should think he must have been impressed with your idea of cold-storage as well, my dear,' Claud raised his glass to her.

'Claud, we're a shocking pair of criminals!' Yvette exclaimed, without any note of repentance.

'Oh come now,' he said with disapproval, 'the man was going to be humiliated and shot. As it is he's done well out of life. Let's hope we taught him a lesson.

'Yvette, we're still young at heart. And we are rich. I don't really want to meet the new owner of the house, whomever he may turn out to be. Come away. They tell me Switzerland is lovely this time of year.'

The Count's Lady

She sat in the apricot morning sunshine, her face hidden by an over-large and well-worn straw hat. Her ample body was neatly dressed in a pale blue flowered cotton dress, and her feet rested half-shod in gay pink espadrilles. A breakfast tray pushed to one end of the table lay covered in crumbs from fresh croissants and a half-finished cup of coffee, the pot of home-made jam, the cracked sugar bowl and mismatched milk pot completed the very picture of someone's holiday breakfast in southern France.

She was writing postcards rather absent-mindedly. It was her custom each year to write all her cards on the first morning so that once she had opened her soul to relaxation there would be nothing to intrude on her self-indulgence.

So now she made brief, cryptic references to weather which would probably be, and villagers whom no doubt she would see. With no date and a pretty picture, what would it matter?

She looked up and gazed about her. From the strip of terrace that extended the length of the house she could look down on the sloping lawn no bigger than a postage stamp which ended abruptly in a hopeless garden beneath an overgrown hedge. At one end of the terrace an iron gate led to the road which rose steeply along the side of the house and up to the village at the top of the hill. Perched as it was, however, the house seemed miles from civilization, only facing out over the gentle, unpopulated hills and patchwork farmland.

It was hard to imagine never seeing these familiar surroundings again after so many happy summers here. Her otherwise cheerful face worked at making a frown. This was the year of her retirement, and after that there would be no extra money for foolish fantasies in France. A housekeeper's pension would be difficult enough to budget for necessities.

With the money she had sensibly put by over the years she would buy a little flat. It wouldn't be the comfortable apartment she had had at Sagewood Hall, but there would be satisfaction in knowing that it was her own. She sighed, remembering the flats she had visited with the estate agent — small, dreary places in cold, faceless streets, where just the look of the stairs made her ache.

She wouldn't think of any of that now. After all, her cards were finished and her holiday had officially begun.

Gardening was the first order of business. In truth it was as much a gesture to let the neighbours know that she was ready to receive visitors as to tidy the beds. She liked the village people with their curious nature and ever-ready gossip. Often their French was too quick for her ear or too distorted by dialect or dental deficiencies to be understood, but long ago she had learned to pass the time agreeably without really saying anything of importance. It was a feeling of pleasant camaraderie with or without the sense of every single word.

Later, in the heat of the day, she would begin on the house. She had come to regard the yearly opening of this rented house as her personal concern. She booked it early each year to be sure that she could see properly to the airing of the linens and the chasing out of winter's traces. The French, she felt, were never thorough.

As with the house, the garden would be put right before her stay was over. It was a treat for her to have morning after warm, sunny morning to work out of doors. The tree in the corner was completely dead this year. She would speak to the Count about having it down. The dear man was probably too busy to have noticed a little detail like that on an insignificant bit of his property.

Although she rented the house through an agency, it was in fact the property of the local Count. His château stood on a nearby rise, hidden from view by the ancient trees of the park which surrounded it. A spire, a magnificent iron gate, a glimpse of a chapel window were all that the imagination was given to play with, that is without boldly trespassing.

The Count himself was not quite such an enigma. He was often in the village chatting with friends in the café, browsing through the market stalls, or just buying his daily loaf of bread. He was lean and straight, and to her his step was just as quick as it had been when he had danced her off her feet at a village fête years before. His hair was still thick but now grey, and his coal black eyes were always full of kind humour. His exaggerated formal manners both charmed and amused her, as he had never dropped his accented, 'My Lady' and she had always responded by calling him '*Monsieur le Comte*' in just as bad French.

They met often during her visits. He was surprised and delighted that she had noticed and taken an interest in the neglected garden. He would stop on his route to ask if everything was as required and would be persuaded to take a cup of coffee and some freshly baked cake. He always protested that he was spoiling her holiday and later a gift of fresh fruit or a box of chocolates would be presented at her door. This of course made a nice excuse to meet again.

In the course of her shopping she might see him sitting outside the café, reading his newspaper, and would join him to take a little white wine. Once they had found themselves taking a meal in the same restaurant and by happy chance had noticed in time to dine together. Today she would go to town to buy some bread and find him to mention the dead tree. She changed her hat and her shoes, and found her basket.

The climb up the hill to the village was steep, but pollarded trees shaded the route right into the village. As she entered the bakery she thought what a luxury it was to buy bread once a day and to spend a few moments just inhaling the warm, yeasty air.

As she left the shop and continued down the street a new shop window caught her eye. An *Immobilier*, an estate agent, had opened an office in the village and his window was full of charming little houses. And what prices! She thought how much nicer her retirement would be in one of these than in some dark, third-floor flat in her grey town at home.

But this was folly. She was much too old to set out alone in a strange country to live. She could only barely speak the language. A holiday was one thing, real life quite another, she told herself sternly. As she was about to take herself along, something caught her eye. For sale in the window was the château of the Count.

The Count stretched one arm out from under the coverlet of the enormous 'boat bed' and found his glasses on the side table. He sat up and peered out of the window into the square below where bright geraniums circled the ancient plane trees and pigeons fluttered and cooed. It was the first day of his holiday, he smiled to himself.

He dressed carefully and went downstairs. His niece was on the terrace reading the morning post. Before her the garden table was laid with the simple but wonderful things of breakfast. He breathed in the smells of coffee and fresh croissants with pleasure and kissed his niece in greeting.

'Your English lady has taken the house for her usual month?' the niece asked with a hint of a smile.

'Yes, so they have told me,' he replied without interest. 'It is the business of the agency.'

'Then I have you for a month,' the niece replied with a smile. 'I do worry now about you living alone. We have so much room and I do enjoy it when you are here.'

He began to feel uncomfortable. It was always like this when he came now. There was room for him to live here, yes, but didn't he notice the absence of his nephew-in-law during his stays? A successful man could not be expected to take on a crumbling, impoverished aristocrat out of charity.

'No, no, my dear,' he patted her hand kindly, 'we shall all remain better friends if I do not. So there it is finished. But I have considered selling my house and settling down in the village, if that will ease your mind.'

'And what of your English lady friend?' the niece teased gently. 'I doubt if she would come if it were not to rent your little house. Tell me, does she know that it is your home the other months of the year?'

'The subject has not come up.' He frowned. 'She thinks that as I am the Count, I must then live in the crumbling château which my father sold years ago. It doesn't matter really but I have said nothing to change these ideas, let us say.

'I have seen a picture of her home in England and that is a *grand château*. I can enjoy her company once a year and live my little dream, can't I? For one month of the year I am the Count of the Château who courts the English Lady of the Manor. There is no harm done, is there?' He smiled merrily as he pleaded mock permission.

His niece laughed, 'Your secret is safe with me.'

'I know,' he finished in devilment, 'because her French is not so good that she would understand what you say anyway.'

He left the house and walked into the busy town where he bought a newspaper and waited for a bus. He enjoyed arriving just below his own little village and walking up to it as if it were the first time he had ever been there.

He was reminded of the first summer when he had rented his house to raise money to help his sister with his niece's education. He had stayed all summer in the loft in his sister's barn.

He had gone himself to call on the tenant, and there he had first seen her, on her knees in the flower-bed, singing to herself. When he had called good-morning, she had started and lost her balance as she tried to get up too quickly. She was without a hat and her delicate complexion was red and blotchy. The next time he called, he brought her a large, wide-brimmed straw hat with his compliments.

Today he strolled into the village and took a seat at the café to read his paper over a cup of coffee and perhaps, as it was the hour for shopping, to meet by accident with his Lady. He knew that the villagers smiled behind his back and so he avoided being seen walking in the direction of her house.

And to him it had become her house. When she left each year it was full of her presence. The garden teemed with flowers and the house was bright from a woman's touch. One year she had suggested tactfully that perhaps the Count might consider new curtains as the old ones made the house look dreary. Explaining that he had no eye for such things and no other woman whose taste he could trust, perhaps the good Lady would be so kind as to choose something herself.

And when the Lady had suggested that a bit of paint here and there might make things more pleasant, and offered to do the decorating herself, he couldn't believe his good fortune. If she were amusing herself and were happy, he had laughed, then she could do with the house as she pleased.

This was, then, the problem. If he sold the house, it would be her house he sold and all the comfort she left with him each year. If he admitted his fraud and tried to arrange another place for her holiday, he knew that nothing would ever be the same. If he were to admit any further interest, it would be unthinkable, even if a bachelor of his age knew where to begin. Perhaps it would not make any difference if he waited just one more year to consider.

Now she was walking past, deep in thought. The Count had to stand and call to her or risk missing her altogether.

'Oh, *Monsieur le Comte*,' she stammered in a pleasant confusion. 'I was in a little dream. I'm sorry. I didn't see you.'

Her French was simple and often she said things in such a funny, turned around fashion that he was either baffled or shocked until he had sorted it out.

'My dear Lady, it is good to see you again. A little glass of wine to celebrate your holiday?' He seated her and ordered.

'And of what were you dreaming this morning?' he asked when they had raised their glasses to each other's health. He led the conversation into English.

'I was thinking how sad it was that you are selling your house,' she began sympathetically.

He choked and tried to compose himself. Was she a mind-reader? '*Pardon?*' was all he could manage to say.

'I noticed the picture of your château in the window of the *Immobilier*,' she explained with gestures, thinking he had misunderstood.

'Oh? Well, it's like that, is it not?' he made casual gestures of unimportance and felt the crisis passing. After all, the château had always been near to ruins, so no wonder its present owners would want to sell it if they could.

'Too big,' she said it as both a statement and a question.

'Yes, yes,' he shook his head, 'you cannot imagine.'

'Yes I can,' she replied. 'It's the same with all big houses, the heating, the insurance...' Taking this opening she continued, 'I plan to move into something smaller myself next year, I think.'

'You are selling your château?' he asked without surprise, as if everyone might be doing so. It was her turn to feel slightly uncomfortable.

'Not exactly,' she hesitated, looking for a graceful escape. 'The others, you know,' she finished with an imitation of the famous French shrug.

'And you will live in your village?' he asked kindly.

'I'm not sure,' her vulnerability broke through for a moment and they were silent.

'It is true. The change is very difficult. I wonder what I will do, too. So we are both starting something new.' He said it as if they were embarking on a picnic and catching his mood she laughed a little and raised her glass in a toast.

'I suppose you might move into the little house that I rent each summer,' she said thoughtfully. How would she tell him she could not come back again?

'But that is impossible,' he said with his eyes twinkling. 'Where would my dear friend spend her holiday and plant her beautiful flowers?'

'I had been thinking,' she paused, unsure whether to voice such a secret, 'of retiring here myself, and buying a little house.' There, it was said.

'But you would leave your friends and family?' he replied in astonishment.

'My dear *Comte*, we must live in between the little time we spend with friends and family. I feel I must choose between making a new life for myself or living as best I can on the fringes of other people's lives.

'And I'm getting too old to enjoy all the travelling. Or maybe I just don't want to any more. Anyway, either I will stay here where I have made friends and can enjoy the sunshine, or I will make a new life in England and say goodbye to lovely France.'

She said all this quite gaily. She thanked the Count for the wine and wished him good-day. He watched as she disappeared down the road into the sunlight as if she were vanishing right there for ever.

'Evenings are always golden here,' she thought as she sat on the terrace. Inky blue-black clouds to the west, however, were coming up quickly, promising a summer storm. The wind turned chill and she went indoors.

The house was of the straightforward plan found in the Gascon countryside everywhere. The front door opened into a central hall and stairway, with two rooms downstairs and two above. Like most gascon houses it faced east with the west side protected from the bad weather.

She had only just begun to think about her supper, falling easily into the French habit of eating well into the evening, after the heat of the day. The kitchen was large and square with a fireplace occupying nearly all of one wall. A fire had been laid in anticipation of her arrival and she lit it, grateful for this bit of thoughtfulness.

There was a sudden knock at the door just as the storm broke. The Count was spared any awkward excuses by the urgency of getting in out of the pelting hailstones.

She motioned him in towards the fire. If she were surprised to see him, she didn't show it. He had brought a bottle of sweet wine to share on the terrace. He laughed as the hailstones bounced everywhere and the thunder rumbled ominously.

She went to find some glasses. 'The French!' she thought in exasperation as all she could find were what looked to be school dinner tumblers. 'They have all the nicest drinks but nothing pretty to drink them from.' As she turned from the cupboard with glasses and a corkscrew, the Count was coming from the door at the back with an armload of wood. She turned a second chair from the central table to face the fire and they sat as he served the wine.

Rain was pattering, gentle and steady now. They watched the fire in silence for a while.

'I have been thinking about our conversation today,' he began, coming to the point of his visit. 'I would never dream of interfering in your affairs, of course,' he added quickly.

'I'm sure that your opinion would be helpful,' she encouraged.

'Are you happy in this house?' he asked bluntly.

'Why, of course. It's like home to me,' she assured him.

'Then if you want to buy a house, I will sell you this house for a low price. Then we can be neighbours in our retirement,' he concluded.

She could think of nothing to say and for a moment she thought she might actually weep.

'That seems like a very good idea,' she managed to say, while looking down at her hands. '*Quelle bonne idée, Monsieur le Comte!*'

'You must call me André now,' he laughed, taking her hand.

'And you must join me for supper,' she replied, feeling that she must do something sensible. 'I've always wished you'd call me Emily, you know.'

'What good ideas you have, Emily,' he said as he sat back to watch the fire with a satisfied smile.

When she had bought the house, he would be rich enough to ask her to consider a more permanent arrangement than just being neighbours.

She smiled as she began making a cheese sauce. When she was

settled they would eat together often and after that, perhaps they would become more than just neighbours. They were now simply two retired people, and what did it matter that he was a count and she only a housekeeper.